# ALL OF YOUR DREAMS WILL COME TRUE WHEN YOU'RE DEAD

JOHN WAYNE COMUNALE

This is a work of fiction. All of the characters, organizations, and events portrayed in this novel are either products of the author's imagination or used fictitiously.



Published by Death's Head Press,
an imprint of Dead Sky Publishing, LLC
Miami Beach, Florida
www.deadskypublishing.com

First U.S. Edition

Cover Art: Justin T. Coons
Edited and Copyedited by: Candace Nola

The "Splatter Western" logo designed
by K. Trap Jones

Book Layout: Lori Michelle
www.TheAuthorsAlley.com

ISBN 9781639511150

SPLATTER
WESTERN

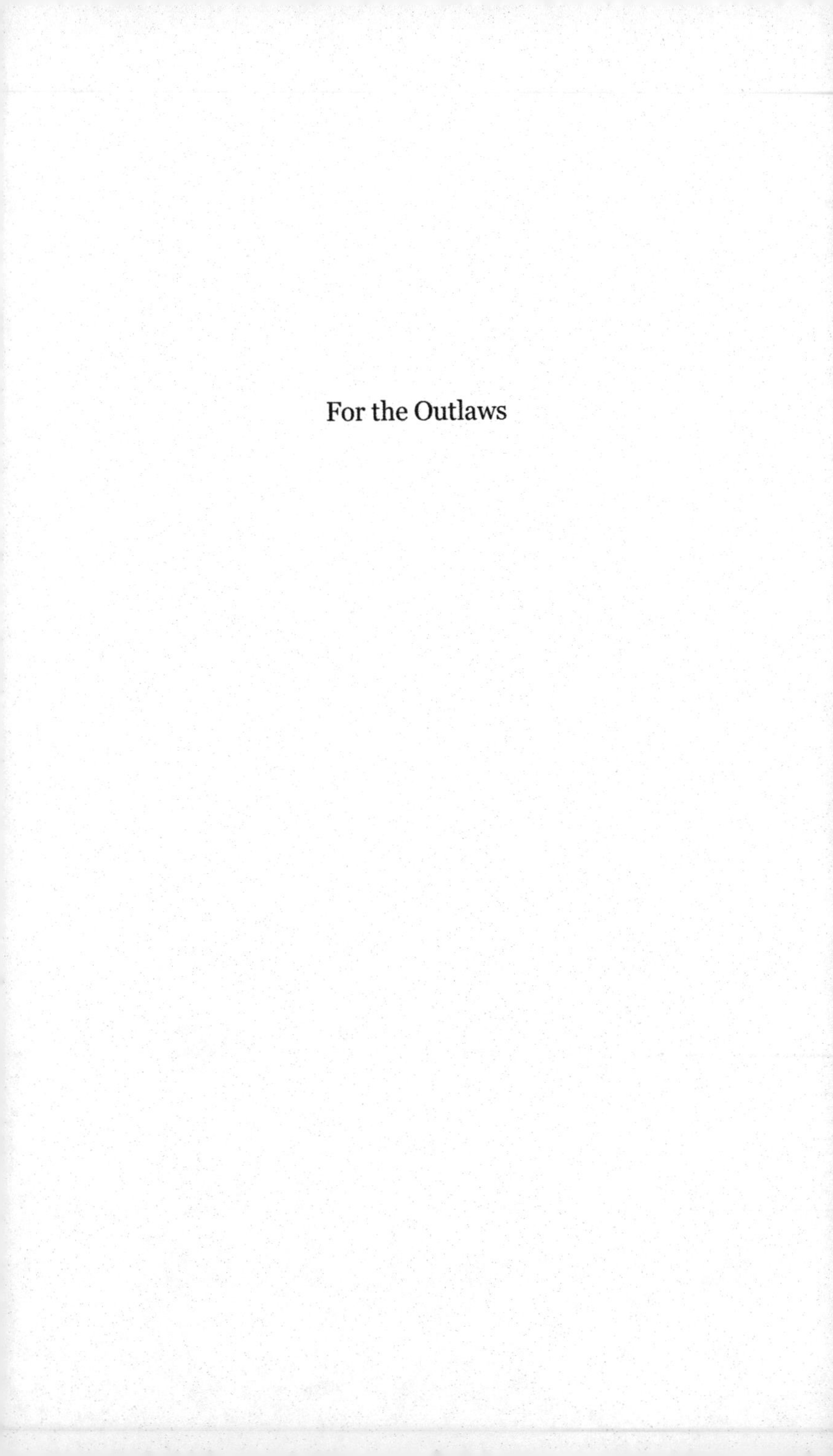

For the Outlaws

# PROLOGUE

COCYTUS WAS A town tucked somewhere in the folds of the never-ending blistering stretch of west Texas desert accessible only to those it chose to call, or rather poach. It was a town you could search for forever and never find or fall ass-backward into without realizing you were there. Of course, by then it's too late. Some say all of your dreams come true when you're dead. The same is said about going to Cocytus, only once there, you may as well be dead, because you're as good as for sure.

Most succumb without resistance, heeding a call only they can discern. A frequency to which only they are tuned. These men are easily taken by darkness, their souls having rotted to fetid filth by the time they reached the place they'd been led, the option of redemption forever off the table upon arrival.

The town was called Cocytus, but that was just fancy talk for *treachery*. The place sucked men in faster than discounted pokes at the local whorehouse and burned them just as badly, only in a different kind of way. Women were taken there as well for different reasons, but none from Cochran.

The cowboys who set off for Cocytus whether by choice or by force were destined for the same fate. They'd be plugged into the grand design, or rather *a* grand design, as another cog churning the further perpetuation of darkness and the irresistible temptations offered as rewards for giving in.

The town's run by a toothy-grinned, manipulative, son-of-a-bitch named Lycus who used a group of prickly snake bandits as enforcers named Luke, Samuel, and Paimon. They called themselves Calamity Three. He kept himself well insulated conducting the majority of his business by way of a young girl he'd turned into a conscious-less marauder of death called Alastor.

The Calamity Three were wanted in every settled state for multiple violent offences and constantly hunted by natives from the different tribes they'd slaughtered for no reason other than to kill. Their sole purpose was to destroy life and hope, to induce *calamity* by way of deployed chaos. They blazed an unstoppable path of havoc across the west with even the best and most seasoned Marshalls unable to bring them in. The fact they ended up in Cocytus with Lycus was destiny playing a cruel joke on every poor soul the three bandits wronged along their way because now, well, they were nearly invincible.

When Luke, Samuel and Paimon joined Lycus and Alastor, the darkest of energy fell across Cocytus, an energy that churned backwards against the current with enough force to change its direction. The three outlaws brought an edge with them that severed the remaining slippery strings of membrane keeping them attached to their present reality. Now, untethered from that world, the bandits slipped through murky quicksand-like ether right into Lycus's control as he allowed them to straddle the line between planes.

The psychic calls started going out directly after the alliance, or at least that was when the men started hearing it. The ones who went easy, the weak ones, began arriving in Cocytus within days sliding seamlessly through an invisible slit smack in the middle of endless desert. The more who came, the farther the darkness was able to reach until there was nowhere it couldn't go.

A small Texas town called Cochran was nestled on the edge of the panhandle where they chose to exist in an ignorance only partially feigned. The men from there who heeded the call all those years ago headed west straight for the desert, each and every one of them, but despite knowing this, not once had a search party been formed to go after them.

The Sheriff, for unknown reasons, was amongst the few men left untouched in the culling of Cochran, though no one knew what, if anything, made these men immune. Despite being unaffected, those left behind were too frightened to go after their friends and family members. They were afraid if they left it would happen to them, and they'd never return. When the Sheriff made the call to not go after the missing men, no one protested.

The people left in town, most of them women and children, did their best to go back to some semblance of normalcy, though the task wasn't easy. The men who could work did their best to help with farming and other labor jobs necessary to keep the town going, but they were spread too thin. Many of the women of Cochran rose to the occasion of stepping in for their absent husband or father, but even that wasn't enough to keep some places from falling into disrepair.

The first few years after the culling were hard, sad, and slow-going, heaping insult upon the injury of an already embittered people. After a few more years things were better, at least comparatively, with the people having finally settled into a relatively comfortable groove. The population had grown to a respectable amount again as a fair number of families were settling in Cochran, and soon the ruined fields became flourishing farms again under the care of new owners with plenty of hands to help.

Those left there during the incident existed with an unspoken agreement to forget about the culling, and to never *never* talk about it. Most of them still harbored their old superstitions, terrified that even mentioning what happened could somehow trigger a second round, one from which the town would not come back. It was something that in any other context would sound ridiculous or childish, but no one in Cochran dared put it to the test.

# HE AIN'T NO GODDAMN SHOOTIST

**LLOYD WAS NO** goddamn shootist. He was a gunfighter, and those are two distinctly different disciplines, worlds apart from each other. Some people, ignorant people, will equate the two citing examples of why and how they're one and the same, but they're dead wrong. A shootist is a sharpshooter, but that doesn't mean they use a rifle exclusively. Some of them could shoot the tick off a bull's ass at a hundred yards with their side iron just as easily.

A shootist has honed a specific kind of practiced patience that keeps them from pulling the trigger too soon. It keeps them cool and calm while they wait for the perfect shot, but sometimes their special kind of patience works against them.

You can wait forever, but the perfect shot isn't worth horseshit if you let your whole party get killed in order to get it. A shootist will always hesitate when it comes time to stand up and shoot from the hip. This doesn't mean they're not brave or good, it means they're not gunfighters.

The shootist is proficient skill-wise but lacks a certain inherent ability a gunfighter is born with. They learn skill and technique the same as anyone, but it's intrinsic talent that sets them apart. It can't be translated tangibly or taught to those who don't have *it*. Trying to put it into words would come off like the incoherent retelling of the fleeting memory of a dream.

It was best described as a feeling.

Gunfighters just started calling it *the touch*, and you had it, or you didn't. Simple as that. Lloyd had the touch, and it didn't take his son, Cherub, long to figure out it'd been passed on to him.

Some stronger-willed men like Lloyd, though few and far between, were able to resist the call, and the Calamity Three would be dispatched to retrieve them. When the bandits stormed into a town atop muscled Mustangs blacker than funeral smoke, they were leaving with who they came for. End of story.

There was something especially unsavory about the Calamity Three. The men radiated a sticky disruptive energy that sent ripples of chaos through every town they went to, some of which would never recover. A town like Cochran didn't stand much of a chance to begin with and had been slowly choking on its own tongue since the culling.

Lloyd didn't end up leaving Cochran with the three dirty, son-of-a-bitch bastards who came to take him to Cocytus, but he ended up there just the same. He couldn't remember how though, only that he was coming around the backside of Jesse's feed and general store to get the drop on the coward bastards looking for him. Gun in hand, he'd turned the corner to come up the side of the building, and that was it. He blinked his eyes and was in a completely different place, with no idea where he was. Lloyd was instantly struck with an overwhelming urgency to get out of this place and back to Cochran, back to his family.

Thing was, he didn't realize how much time had actually passed since he'd been gone. What felt like seconds had been years, though Lloyd hadn't aged, nor did he perceive the elongated passage of time, and nothing about his current surroundings indicated as much. Time operated differently in Cocytus and the linear perception of the concept did not exist within its borders, but he'd yet to figure that out.

# ALL OF YOUR DREAMS WILL COME TRUE

Lloyd looked around the unfamiliar town and walked out to the road, stepping over the trail of horse hoof divots. The building he'd found himself next to was a general store as well, only it wasn't Jesse's and appeared to be closed or abandoned. Down the street, he saw what looked like a bank with a water trough out front, directly across the street from another bank with a similar trough. He thought it odd for a town to have two banks.

There were no horses tied out front of either building or any other building as far down as he could see. Lloyd cocked his head and strained his ear trying to detect the rhythmic clomp of a trotting Philly or thunderous gallop of approaching Mustangs, but he'd be goddamned if he could hear a thing. The silence gave the impression he may be in a ghost town, but the buildings were too well maintained to have been abandoned. Unless it happened recently.

Lloyd moved slowly down the wood plank sidewalk to get a better look and found they weren't banks at all, they were gambling halls. He'd heard the government was enacting a national anti-gambling law, but it clearly hadn't made it this far south yet. A big change like that would require a good amount of time to take hold and be enforced across the country. Having *two* gambling halls when you're not supposed to have any was like swinging a pair of big brass balls in Uncle Sam's face. It was asking for trouble.

He continued down past a saloon, finding it empty as well. From the sidewalk, looking over the swinging doors, he could see full bottles of hooch on the shelves and clean glasses lined up across the bar. He'd have figured to at least find a lone barman whose ear he could bend with the growing number of questions he had. *Where was he? Where was everyone else? Why the hell was he here?*

Lloyd continued past the saloon for a better view of the sign on the building he'd mistaken for a bank, though to be fair large dollar signs painted in gold flanked both sides of the door.

"Co—Cy—Tus Gambling Hall," he read out loud. "What the hell's a Cocytus?"

"Not what, but where."

The voice came from behind, and Lloyd spun, drawing and leveling his iron at whoever thought it was a good idea to sneak up on him. A cowboy stood in the shadow just outside the swinging saloon doors. He was thin and wiry with a dusty flat-brimmed hat and an ill-fitting leather vest over a clingy threadbare shirt. He smoked a thin cigar in tiny puffs as his eyes wandered across the buildings on the other side of the street.

Something was wrong. Lloyd had drawn his gun, but it *wasn't* in his hand. It wasn't hanging off his hip either, but he kept pawing at the empty holster like it would suddenly appear.

"Wha—What in the hell is th—"

"It's not a thing, it's a place," the stranger said, still smoking while looking across the street and not at Lloyd. "Cocytus. It's a place. It's the place you're in right now."

"What the hell'd you do with my gun!?!"

The question, though more of a demand, took priority over everything else, but the stranger looked on, puffing his cigar. Lloyd couldn't give a good goddamn anymore about where, when, or why until the pistol was back in his hand. Lloyd's gun hadn't been out of his possession since he'd taken it off another gunfighter whilst passing through a small, East-Texas, cattle town close to nine years ago. The thing had become a part of him, and his palm ached over its absence.

The other gunfighter was just a kid really, with a mouth bigger than he could control and more gun than he knew how to handle. Lloyd only stopped to water his horse and hadn't planned on conducting any other business, not even a drink for himself, until the kid stepped out of the saloon across the street. He stared Lloyd down with whiskey-bleared eyes and yelled something about 'recognizing' him, and 'knowing what he did'. Before Lloyd could say he was mistaken, the kid's hand was already dancing around the butt of the gun on his hip. He was nervous though, and Lloyd could see him shaking from across the street.

He didn't think it would come to it, hoped it wouldn't, but Lloyd pulled aside the filthy poncho he wore when traveling to show he was indeed prepared. He figured it would slow the kid down a bit, give him a moment to think about what he was doing before he did it, but it only invigorated his resolve.

"I don't know who you think I am," Lloyd called, "but I ain't them."

Truth be told, it actually *could* have been him the kid was looking for since those goddamn wanted posters would get around from time to time, but he didn't think it was possible for someone to recognize him from across the street. Perhaps there was something in his posture or profile? Maybe the way he carried himself sparked a forgotten memory of someone from the kid's past who'd wronged him. Someone he very clearly did not like.

"Don't tell me, you lyin' son-of-a—"

The kid went to pull his gun but by that time he was already shot. The placement was a hair to the left, but the bullet still struck his heart cleanly, killing him before he'd had a chance to realize he was dead. Lloyd holstered his iron and walked to where the kid dropped in the street, but paused when he was close enough to see the dead man's weapon. It was still in the holster, but Lloyd recognized it from the handle alone.

He moved closer and bent to remove it to be sure he wasn't mistaken. He was not. The gun the kid never got a chance to draw on Lloyd was a LeMat revolver. He'd only ever seen one of them in his life, and that was years ago. The French-made pistol held nine rounds instead of six and came fitted with a second wider barrel loaded with buckshot.

The gun was originally manufactured for and issued to the confederacy but nearly all of them were confiscated and destroyed by the Union blockade. The ones that survived were either taken from dead men on the battlefield, or secretly kept by union soldiers who were supposed to destroy them. The weapon was coveted by gunfighters and shootists alike, and somehow one ended up in the hands of a kid with no concept of what he had.

Lloyd turned the LeMat over, examining the thing like it came from another planet before wrapping his fingers around the handle. The finish didn't show the gun's age, as it clearly never saw much use. The weight was perfectly balanced, and it felt good in his hand, like it'd been made just for him. Lloyd hadn't used anything aside from his Colt Peacemaker leading up to that day, and it'd served him well, saving his life more times than he cared to count. After holding the LeMat though, the Colt felt foreign and awkward, even slippery. He didn't need time to think about it, as there was no doubt Lloyd would be using the LeMat from there on out.

He heard shuffling and looked up to see the heads of three men peering out from over the saloon door, but none made a move to come outside. Lloyd stared them down, able to tell what they were thinking from the looks on their faces. They weren't looking for trouble and just wanted him to get on his horse and leave. Men like this were typically branded as cowards, but Lloyd preferred to think of them as smart for valuing their own lives.

He bent back over the kid to take his gun belt and holster but kept the LeMat in his hand and one eye on the men in the saloon in case one of them came down with a sudden case of courage. Lloyd slung the belt over his shoulder and walked backwards across the street to his horse, keeping a steely eye leveled at the saloon. He climbed in the saddle, snapped the reins, and rode back out into the surrounding wilderness.

Lloyd was still holding the LeMat as he galloped off, and it stayed in his hand for the majority of the ride. He didn't shoot it until he stopped that night to camp in one of the valleys of the sprawling hill country. The gun felt like an extension of himself, like it was psychically connected to his brain. He was rapt with tremendous pleasure when he pulled the trigger, not in a sexual way but a satisfying euphoria along the same lines. Unlike sex, Lloyd wasn't left spent and sluggish. He felt charged and alert, like all of his senses had been turned up a notch, keenly tuning him into everything going on around him.

Since then, he'd kept the LeMat on him at all times. He even slept with it and took it with him to the jakes. Not having it all of a sudden filled Lloyd with a distress growing increasingly dire by the second coupled with a creeping anxiety, both of which fueled his temper. If he didn't have the LeMat back in his hand in the next two seconds, he was going to rip the stranger's head off with his bare hands. Lloyd repeated his demand with ratcheting fury and took a step toward the cowboy.

"I said, where's my gun? You hear me! WHERE!"

"Gun?" The stranger's cool, relaxed tone matched his posture as he leaned against the doorframe, finally looking at Lloyd. "They took your gun; they take everyone's gun. Count yourself lucky that was all they took. So far, at least."

This was not the answer he wanted, and Lloyd could hear his heartbeat pound in his ears as his blood pressure rose in matched pace with his anger. He charged the stranger, seizing his vest before pulling him in close. The cigar remained clenched in his teeth, dangling from the side of the man's mouth, his reaction smug and nonplussed.

"Relax, partner," the stranger said. "They'll give you a chance to win it back."

"*Win* it back? You better start making some goddamn sense, and I ain't your goddamn *partner* neither!"

Lloyd pushed the stranger hard against the wall, and this time the cigar dropped. He stood back, ready for the man to retaliate, but all he did was smile. A beat of silence passed between the two before the stranger bent over to retrieve the cigar. He brought it to his mouth and puffed the dying cherry back to life.

"What's your name?" asked the man.

"What the hell difference does that make? I want my damn LeMat!"

"What's your name?" The stranger repeated himself, slow and easy.

"It's Lloyd, goddamn-it!"

"Lloyd," the stranger tipped his hat. "Lloyd, like I was saying before, you're in Cocytus. Things don't work the same here as they do other places you've been. Huffin' and puffin' don't get you nowhere, you see; might don't make right in Cocytus. You'd best learn the rules before you go doing somethin' you'll . . . regret."

Lloyd wasn't interested in whatever game the strange cowboy was playing, but he was sharp enough to know when the chips were stacked against him and how to act accordingly. He had no gun, no horse, no idea where he was, and not another soul, save the stranger, around to ask. He was going to have to go along with it until another opportunity presented itself to him, but once he had the LeMat in his hands again, the cowboy was as good as dead.

"What are the 'rules', then?" Lloyd struggled to keep his voice low and steady. "Here in Cocytus."

"Well," the stranger paused to smoke, "you gotta *learn* the rules. I can't just come out and tell you. Like I said, things work differently here."

If he was trying to pull another reaction out of Lloyd, he was doing one hell of a job, but the missing weight of the LeMat on his hip reminded him to stay composed.

"Any advice on where to start? You said *they* would give me a chance to win my gun back, so who's 'they' and what's the game?"

"That ain't none of my concern or business." The stranger was looking across the street again, his eyes aimed at the gambling hall. "But you'll most likely find the answers in there. Most likely."

“The gambling hall? I don’t even have any money on me. What am I supposed to gamble with?”

“They’ll figure out something, always do.”

The cowboy leaned back against the doorframe again and smoked while Lloyd examined the entrance to the hall. The large gold dollar signs shimmered in the reflected sunlight, and he noticed for the first time there were no windows in the building. There weren’t windows in any of the buildings. The swinging doors of the saloon offered the only opportunity to see inside of anywhere so far. He looked the street up and down one more time hoping to see signs of activity, another person from which he might get a more detailed description of what exactly the hell was happening.

Lloyd shot a glance over his shoulder at the cowboy, but he was staring off again, watching the smoke he exhaled swirl away in the breeze. He touched the empty holster strapped to his side and his vigor renewed as he approached the Cocytus Gambling Hall directly across the street from a second identical Cocytus Gambling Hall.

Lloyd wondered why the man sent him to one over the other, and when he turned to ask, the stranger called out.

“Hey Lloyd.”

A long silence passed between them until Lloyd finally yelled back.

“Well? What?”

“Good luck.”

The stranger flicked what was left of the cigar into the street and disappeared back through the swinging doors.

# CHERUB

**HIS NAME WAS CHARLIE**, but he'd been called Cherub on account of his chubby cheeks framed by soft golden curls sprouting from an unfortunately oversized head. He eventually grew into his head, got tall and slim, and while his hair remained a dusty colored blonde, it grew long and straight just past his shoulders. While his physical appearance eventually changed, the name didn't, and Charlie was known only as Cherub through adolescence and into adulthood.

His dad never called him by the nickname though and was, in fact, the only person who called him Charlie. It was hard for Cherub to remember exactly what the man looked like, but his mother, Emma, had a picture to remind him. She kept the old photograph, gone yellow and brittle with age, beside the bed she slept in alone, at least for a little while, and when Cherub thought about his father, this was the face he saw in his head.

He caught his mother talking to it sometimes, the picture, other times she would hold it to her chest and cry. This is how he knew his father's name was Lloyd because it was the only word he could make out between her sobs. She never told Cherub why he left but would only say 'he was a good man. Misunderstood, but good'.

His father was one of the last to go in the culling, but as far as most folks in town were concerned, holding out the longest didn't warrant adulation. Cherub was too young when it happened, he had no grasp on what was going on or why it was so impactful to the town, and like other children around his age at the time he wouldn't be told much.

Cherub knew his dad's name was Lloyd, knew he was a gunfighter, and knew he was gone. That was the extent of it, and he imagined all the kids were told some variation of the same story. Any questions he asked were answered with a backhand across the face, so he learned to live with the limited amount of information he'd been given.

Lloyd was no farmer, so that kind of physical labor wasn't something Cherub had to worry about taking up. His father was a gunfighter just like his mother told him. He wasn't and never had been a bandit, or at least that was the way he told it to his wife. He wasn't one to go around looking for trouble necessarily, but what she didn't know wouldn't hurt her.

The problem was more often than not, trouble found Lloyd; it found him again and again and again. This was how he'd discovered at a young age he had what people call a natural inclination for gun fighting, which served him well since the trouble that found Lloyd usually came with a loaded pistol pointed his way.

He took good care of his family before he was taken away into the mysterious darkness. Lloyd had always been able to come up with the money needed to finance their humble but happy life on a small plot of land in Cochran. Sometimes he'd have to leave town for a few days at a time to 'work', but he always came back with enough money to keep them high on the hog for a month at least.

Emma didn't ask her husband any questions about his 'work', and he didn't volunteer any information on the topic. The two of them never sat down to hash out an understanding, as it wasn't something they needed to discuss verbally. They'd had the conversation with their eyes a thousand times at least, and the outcome was always the same.

Cherub was nine when he found the gun. Nine and a

half, really. It was a Colt Single Action Army Revolver technically but was more commonly referred to as a 'Peacemaker'. Cherub didn't know any of those details presently, but in time he'd come to forget more about guns than most so-called experts learn in their lifetime. It just came to him naturally, as naturally as it came to Lloyd.

Cherub found the old Colt with a holster and belt full of bullets shoved between where the wall met the ceiling near the far corner of the barn on the backside of their property. It was doorless and rotting since his father had no use or desire to keep the structure maintained and allowed it to fall into disrepair, ever teetering on the verge of collapse. The barn wasn't safe for anyone to be inside, especially an unsupervised nine-year-old boy, but Cherub's mother was in the throes of addiction by this point and quite unavailable to offer any guidance.

Emma loved her son. She loved him with all her heart, but morphine has a way of distorting the way love is expressed. Cherub never begrudged his mother. He loved her back in the best way he knew how.

It didn't take long for the money to run out once Lloyd was gone, and that's when Emma turned to whoring. The land they lived on was lousy with rocks, and the small patches of soil that did exist were rife with clay nowhere fit for farming. Cherub was too young to work and, given Lloyd's reputation, the family didn't have any friends to fall back on for help. Selling a poke was the easiest way for Emma to support the two of them, and she was still young enough to draw a decent nightly take at that.

She stayed at the hotel in town part-time, which was what they called the four rooms above Slim Whitley's saloon, where she and the other ladies turned tricks. Slim was among the few men still in town after the culling, though no one would've missed him had he been taken. Whores with kids weren't good for business, so Cherub spent a lot of time in the house alone from the time he was still pissin' his britches. He grew up fast though, had to if he wanted to survive.

The time his mother spent at the brothel quickly overtook the amount spent at home, going from a few hours a night to being gone for days. One or two times her absence spanned over a week and Cherub thought he'd finally been abandoned, not that he didn't feel he'd been already. When Emma was home, she slept and cried and slept some more before going back to Slim's. Eventually, she stopped checking on Cherub altogether, going straight to bed instead.

Cherub didn't know how she could stay in there so long without food or water, but he wasn't intimately familiar with the behavior of a morphine addict yet. Otherwise, he would've known right away. It started one night at the hotel when a visiting cowboy employed Emma for her services, then up and passed out cold on top of her mid-poke. It took longer than she'd have liked to maneuver out from under the limp bulk form he'd become, and twenty excruciating minutes later she was plenty riled up because of it.

She got dressed and set to smacking the naked stranger on the back of the head, and while he didn't move, he did start to snore, and loudly. Emma reared back to smack him again when her eye landed on the dusty saddlebag the cowboy laid on the floor beside the bed. She'd seen him bring it up to the room but thought nothing of it until now. Emma dove onto the bag and impatiently yanked at the strap and buckle until composing herself enough to slowly separate the two.

She reached inside and her hand came back, clutching a banded stack of confederate bills that hadn't held value in over fifteen years. She cursed and slung the stack at the sleeping cowboy's snoring face. The telltale jingle of coins sent her digging for the pouch or purse they'd be in, which she quickly found and removed. She loosened the strings, emptied it into her palm, and smiled down at the four gold coins she now held. They were called 'Liberty Heads', or at least she'd heard them called that, and while Emma didn't know their exact value, gold was always worth something to somebody. She slid the coins into the secret pocket of her corset and shuffled through what was left in the bag.

Among the remaining contents were two silver notes worth a dollar each, and one five-dollar gold note issued by a bank in Oklahoma she'd never heard of. Not everyone had them yet, but Emma knew federal 'greenbacks' were taking over as the national currency and had already seen a few of the new bills pass through Slim's hands downstairs. If the gold and silver notes weren't already as worthless as the confederate bills, they would be soon and were of no use to her.

A small brown bottle was left at the bottom amongst loose bullets and other worthless papers. It was corked uptight, but she worked it back and forth until it was loose enough to pull. The sharp sweet smell curled up and hooked to her nostrils, and now Emma knew exactly why the cowboy fell into sudden hibernation. The liquid within was morphine diluted by strong whiskey or gin, or more commonly known as laudanum. It was billed and sold as a miracle cure-all, and while some of Slim's other girls used the drug from time to time, Emma didn't have extra money to spend on possible snake oil and never tried it herself.

The cock-sure cowboy must've been sipping from the bottle between drinks downstairs, and both ships crashed on top of him at once resulting in his current unconscious state. The poor bastard knocked his own dick in the dirt before it had a chance to get out the gate.

Emma re-corked the bottle, buried it deep in the space between her breasts, and got to her feet. She left the man there and went back downstairs, hoping to sell a couple more pokes before the night was through. It'd be harder now since she'd wasted so much time already, but she'd pulled off miracles in the past. Maybe tonight she was due one.

Downstairs, she found the saloon crowd had thinned out considerably and realized more time passed than she'd thought. A group of four dusty ranch hands who'd come to Cochran after hearing there was plenty of work sat beneath a silvery translucent cloud of tobacco smoke in the corner playing cards. They wouldn't be done anytime soon, nor would any of them be fit for a poke when they were, so Emma planted herself on a stool at the end of the bar to sulk. If not for the coins she'd taken from the cowboy's bag, the night would've been a complete bust.

She set her elbows on the bar with her head in her hands and felt something cold and smooth rub against her skin. She went to adjust her corset and remembered the bottle she'd hidden in her cleavage. A quick, surreptitious glance around showed Slim with his back to her watching the card game while the men at the table watched their cards. No one saw her fingers dip quickly between her cinched bosom to fish out the bottle. The cork came off easier this time, and Emma gave a silent toast to the memory of her Lloyd before taking the first sip on her way to ruin.

Cherub had been out to the barn countless times and couldn't believe he hadn't found the gun sooner. He often spent time there for no reason other than to be out of the house, as it offered a change of scenery and a fresh perspective. The barn was an escape where he could let his overactive imagination conjure invisible friends with which to play games.

He would pretend to chase wanted bandits through the wilderness, a game that always ended in a shoot-out where Cherub expertly dispatched the bad guys using a gun made up of his thumb and forefinger. Sometimes when his mother was walking the line between pleasantly high and too stoned to move, she'd take Cherub into town with her where he'd see guns hanging from hips of cowboys but never held one in his hand until he found the Colt.

His inclusion on these outings was infrequent,

invariably ending with Emma forgetting she'd brought the boy along only to react violently upon realizing he was in tow. She might've directed her emotions at Cherub, but she knew the anger driving it was misplaced. Emma wasn't angry at Cherub for tamping down her high, or being under foot, or for any other reason. She was angry at herself for what she was putting him through, what she was putting both of them through. He'd lost his father before he was old enough to form a solid memory of the man, and in her attempt to shoulder the burden alone, Cherub lost her too.

She didn't know any other way to express her frustration with herself and their situation other than screaming at Cherub while whooping him stupid. It was easy for Emma to fall into the morphine habit because it let her forget, temporarily suspending her emotions by way of poison euphoria. Each hit reset the clock on her time-bomb of sadness, but the fuse grew shorter, requiring a continuous increase in dosage to further belie the explosion. She didn't know which would give out first, her mind or her body, only that they both would, and soon.

Emma wanted to get better, wanted to *be* better for her son. She just had no idea how. Cherub's love for his mother never faltered despite being made her whipping boy. She was rarely cognizant enough to know he was there, but when she did, Cherub received the full brunt of her festering melancholy. The fact he didn't hold any of this against her made it worse, and she began resenting him for *not* being angry with her, for not hating her the way she hated herself.

According to Emma's memory, which was riddled with gaps from vice, she'd never told Cherub much of anything about his father. She'd told him Lloyd was a good man, that he was strong, a fighter, and leaving it at that. She didn't want Cherub knowing about the kind of fighting his father did on account she didn't want him getting any ideas about following in Lloyd's footsteps, or worse, feel obligated to. Emma entertained her husband in his non-verbal insistence on secrecy, letting him believe she truly had no idea what he really did when he'd leave town to 'work'.

Lloyd was serious and tight-lipped on the subject, but after having his perspective doused in whiskey, his attitude would change. Truth was, there'd been many a night when Lloyd would tell his wife stories of his gun fighting exploits, the money he'd won or stolen, the men he'd killed. He told her everything, only bourbon stole any memory he had of doing it, and Emma never reminded him. She was sure he had his reasons, and they made sense to him, so she let him have them without questioning his motives. Besides, she didn't take moral issue with what Lloyd had to do for his family.

Unbeknownst to Emma, she'd been parroting this very behavior with Cherub. In the early days of her addiction before things got bad; before she'd made the switch from sipping laudanum to uncut morphine. Before she'd taken up the needle. Some nights Emma would come home lucid. Stoned, but lucid and chatty, and what she chatted about was Lloyd to the only other person in the house, Cherub.

Her ability to tell the stories varied according to the intensity of her altered state, but he remained rapt with attention hanging on every slurred mumble stumbling awkwardly out of her mouth. Cherub listened to those stories no matter how many times she'd repeat them, committing each and every detail to memory. The next day Emma would remember nothing about the conversation, and like his mother before him, Cherub didn't dare remind her. Doing so would break the spell, so to speak, and the stories would stop.

It didn't matter, since the stories stopped on their own when Emma's habit took over another sprawling swath of her life. Cherub savored everything he learned about his father in that small window of time, and as his mother feared, he'd instantly begun romanticizing the man's life, the life of a gunfighter.

It was a life Cherub wanted as well. He wanted his *own*

life only it would be a long time before he'd be given a chance, if given one at all. His mother wouldn't teach him gun fighting even if she could, and there wasn't anyone else in his life to ask. If Cherub had any uncles or cousins, he didn't know them, and no other family *or* friends had ever come to visit. It was just the two of them, and lately, more and more, it was just him.

Cherub didn't know how much time he'd spent staring down at the gun where he'd set it on the ground, but could tell the sun had moved some by the position of his shadow. He wasn't thinking so much as he was watching vivid vignettes play across his mind's eye of what his life would be like with a pistol in hand. Everything would change, and opportunities previously inaccessible would be wide open. He'd have to teach himself to shoot, but he had nothing but time and a whole heap of patience. He could be a gunfighter just like his father, maybe even better.

By the time Cherub decided to pick up the gun, he found it was already in his hand.

# CALAMITY COMES HOME

**THE CALAMITY THREE** weren't sure what happened to the horses they arrived in Cocytus with but had no complaints about the eyeless demonic beasts they'd been replaced with. They were a gift from Lycus after they'd agreed to work with him, though they hardly considered the man their 'boss'. Authority held no sway with Samuel, Luke, and Paimon, who could never be controlled no matter how much money, horses, or whores you threw at them.

While Lycus provided the men with an abundance of both, it didn't change the way they felt about being told what to do. They'd go along with Lycus's plan for as long as they stood to benefit, but once that changed, there would be no keeping Calamity in Cocytus. If Lycus had a problem, they'd just kill him like they had every other living thing attempting to impose its will upon the bandits. They answered to no one, including each other.

These are the kind of men who would sooner slice their own mother's neck than obey the simplest of orders if they hadn't already killed them, of course. Their mothers officially died during childbirth due to complications and blood loss, as it was unfortunate but not uncommon for massive hemorrhaging to occur during a breech birth. The truth was, they tore their way out of the womb, ripping through organs and flesh to free themselves. They entered the world on their own terms. Men like this were the lowest of the low, which was what made them so dangerous.

The Calamity Three were loyal to no one, but Lycus

knew that going in. He knew a lot about them. He knew they'd arrive in Cocytus long before they had, and that the three men would be integral in the hastening of the end. Lycus planned to use the concentrated darkness of Cocytus to bring Behemoth over from Oblivion. The mammoth's presence would bring an unstoppable chaos with it, and if Lycus had everything lined up on his end, Oblivion would be forcibly yanked through. More importantly, Lycus would finally be home, where he would make the world end and start again in the distorted reality of Cocytus.

First, Lycus needed to weigh the town down with dark souls, dense and thick, heavy enough to help Behemoth tear through the fabric of time. The souls required needed to come from particular men, ones with a special kind of corrupting selfishness. There were many selfish men in the world, but the ones Lycus needed had to be cutthroat in their pursuit, uncompromising and wholly consumed by the trait. It had to define them.

The psychic signal sent out by Alastor brought most of them right to Cocytus and allowed them to slip between the two planes of existence the town was hidden between. Alastor was Lycus's right hand-woman, his muscle and protégé in one. She'd always had certain psychic abilities, talents really, but she'd never have known it if Lycus hadn't helped coax the skills out of her. He showed her how to use and strengthen her gift, and she took to it quickly, far outpacing the progress he'd expected in a short amount of time. She was a natural.

Things were a bit bristly between Alastor and the Calamity Three, but she had good reason to keep her guard up. She sensed an air of betrayal from them and knew they could turn on Lycus at any time for any reason. He assured her he was already well aware of what the Calamity Three were capable of, and when it came time, *he* would take care of it, but she couldn't help being concerned. The bandits didn't trust Lycus, let alone his sidekick, which was just as well since Alastor had trust issues herself.

# THE LITTLE GIRL IN THE DESERT

LYCUS WASN'T HER father, but the closest thing she had to one. If she had parents, Alastor didn't know them, and the way Lycus talked made it seem like she'd been hatched from an egg, or suddenly popped into existence. Thing was, she believed him. Alastor believed everything Lycus told her, and why shouldn't she? The man raised her up and was the only other person in her life. What the Calamity Three lacked in loyalty and trust, Alastor made up for in spades when it came to Lycus. Aside from him, not a single other life mattered, and she was fiercely protective of the man who'd saved her.

She couldn't remember very far back, but Lycus told her he'd found her wandering alone through a patch of West-Texas desert with the nearest town a half day's ride away. Said she couldn't've been more than five-years-old at the time. There wasn't anyone else around far as he could tell, and when he asked what her name was and how she got there, he was answered with the blank stare of a mute.

Lycus pulled the girl up onto his horse and told her to hold tight. He arrived in town with her a few hours later and asked anyone he came upon in the street if they knew who the girl belonged to, but none did. He was reluctant to go to the Sheriff not only because of his distrust of lawmen, but there was a chance Lycus might be recognized, and not for being a popular fellow either. He'd never been on the right side of the law, and sometimes his reputation would precede him. He watered and fed his horse, then the two shared a meal of beef stew and corn biscuits at the saloon that doubled as a boarding house. They ate in silence, her unable to speak and him deep in thought.

The sun was starting to tuck itself behind the desert horizon, sending an explosion of pink and purple across the sky in preparation for the coming night. Lycus put her on the horse before climbing on himself. He reluctantly started them down the street in the direction of the sheriffs, but pulled the reins and stopped short by a hundred feet or so. He could feel her trembling with fear before he leaned over to speak softly in her ear.

"This isn't the way for you," he said. "You deserve better than this, and that is exactly what I'm going to give you."

Lycus snapped the reins and dug his heels into the side of his horse sending them sprinting past the sheriff's station and out of town where the darkness of the treacherous Texas wilderness swallowed them whole. She'd already been asleep in the saddle for a while before Lycus finally stopped and made camp next to an outcropping of tall rocks. He tended his horse before laying out the bedroll for her, and within moments, she was right back to sleep. He imagined she hadn't had any type of good rest since she'd gotten separated from or abandoned by her family.

It was too late to bother with a fire, but he prepped one for the morning so no time would be wasted. He used his saddle as a pillow and laid across from the girl falling asleep almost as quickly as she had. They'd been riding for a while and there weren't many hours left for shuteye by the time they stopped, but the two of them squeezed in every second of sleep before the sun returned to hold the night at bay for another twelve hours or so.

## ALL OF YOUR DREAMS WILL COME TRUE

In the morning, Lycus heated water over the fire to make coffee for himself, then ripped a piece of pan de campo off for the girl and handed it to her. She examined the bread cautiously before taking a bite, and upon finding the first taste palatable, ate the rest without hesitation.

"You gotta name?"

It was the first words Lycus had spoken to her since riding out of town the night before, realizing too late that if she did, there'd be no way to tell him. She stared back across the fire at him, chewing a mouthful of bread.

"I don't suppose you know how to write either?"

This time, the girl slowly shook her head before popping the last bit of camp bread into her mouth.

"Didn't figure as much," he said, ripping his own serving in half, passing it over the fire to her. "You remind me of someone I used to know, come to think of it. Name was Alastor, he was a sneaky fellow and real quiet too. How about I call you Alastor?"

The edges of the girl's lips curled up nearly imperceptibly but was the closest expression approximating a smile she'd shown since Lycus found her.

"You like that, huh?" He paused for a moment to think before continuing. "I reckon you could go by Alice though, you being a girl and all."

She bristled at this, shaking her head with more fervor than before. She liked the name 'Alastor' as soon as he'd said it and didn't feel the need to compromise because of her gender. Names held power, and she felt it in the one he'd given her.

"Okay, okay, Alastor it is," he said, putting his hands up in mock surrender. "Suits you better anyway. You're no 'Alice'."

Her smile returned, undeniably this time, and Lycus couldn't help but smile back. He didn't know where this little girl came from, or where she was supposed to be, but there was a reason he found her.

Lycus had told her the story of how he'd found her

enough times she could recite it verbatim if she were able to speak. It was a pleasant enough story, but not a word was true. He didn't find Alastor; he took her, and when he discovered she held the key to bringing his plan to fruition, Lycus made sure she could *never* go back.

# THE SOUTHPAW PATH

CHERUB TOOK TO practicing his shooting every day, even a couple times a day when he could. It wasn't hard keeping it from his ma, as she'd taken to spending longer stretches of time at the 'hotel' and was in an opiate fog the few times she did come home. He honestly didn't know why she bothered anymore since she never stayed long, her focus having shifted completely from caring for her son to feeding her addiction. She took the lantern with her the last time she'd been there, leaving Cherub to rely on candlelight to see at night from then on.

The hard part was trying to figure out how he'd get more cartridges once the ones held by the gun belt were gone. Wasn't much of a point to practice shooting if he ran out of ammo soon as he started. The first thing he did was scavenge the rickety barn for any other rounds that might be hidden or possibly fallen loose. His efforts lauded a single cartridge he discovered in the corner, half buried in dirt and mouse shit. It wasn't until Cherub searched the house that he found what he needed to sustain his training.

He'd become suspicious of a creaking floorboard in his mother's room and pulled it up to find what amounted to a small armory's worth of cartridges. He figured his dad had been hiding them there a little at a time, storing them away so he'd never be in a pinch for rounds. There was no way his mother had known they were hidden down there, or she'd taken them to town to trade for morphine or Laudanum or both.

Cherub didn't think she'd be able to find them now, but just the same, he put the cartridges in a bucket and hid them out in the barn. The Colt, he hid beneath the thin mattress on the floor in his room where he slept. He liked for it to be close to him; it felt good, right. If he was going to be a gunfighter like his father, he was pretty sure it meant he'd have to be within reach of his gun at all times. He figured he might as well get used to it.

The number of cartridges looked less impressive in the bucket than when he'd found them in the floor, but there was still a whole hell of a lot of them, and he was determined to make every last one count. It was a promise he'd made to himself before squeezing the trigger for the first time, one he knew he'd have no trouble keeping. Cherub held the gun out in front of him, one eye squinting down the barrel as he tried to aim from an arm's length away. He pointed it at an old stump behind the barn about ten feet from him and pulled the trigger. The Colt kicked hard, and he nearly dropped it, his shot flying wildly off target.

He thought his wrist might be broken, but a quick check confirmed he was overreacting. Cherub shook out his wrist and attempted to adjust his grip on the handle, but decided instead to switch the gun from his right hand to his left. He fired again and still missed his target but not as widely to the right this time, and while prepared for the kick, it didn't feel as strong. No, it was that he had more control with his left hand, more power.

Cherub pulled the trigger a third time and was momentarily startled when a chunk of stump exploded into splintery pulp. His ears rang, and he smiled despite his jumpiness. By the end of the day, the stump was in pieces.

# THE ENGLISHMAN

**LLOYD PULLED THE** door to the gambling hall, and it opened easily for being as big as it was. He stuck his head into the darkness beyond the threshold, and his skepticism was renewed by the lack of light and sound coming from within. Lloyd turned to look back out at the empty space left by the stranger again before he shook his head and stepped inside.

"Goddamn crazy bastard. This ain't nothin' like no gambling hall I ever been to before."

The door closed behind him, and Lloyd searched his pockets for matches he already knew weren't there. It smelled like wet soil and pine inside, which reminded Lloyd a little too much of the freshly built caskets outside the funeral parlor in Cochran.

"Goddamn! Goddamnit!"

A light snapped on at the end of the long hallway he didn't realize he was standing in until now.

"What the hell kind of a place—"

"Mr. Lloyd, I presume," came a voice from below the light.

Lloyd squinted in the direction it came from until his eyes adjusted enough for him to see the blond-haired man in a fancy three-piece suit with a finely manicured mustache curled up at the sides with wax. He spoke in a proper British accent, and Lloyd ached to answer the man with his LeMat, balling his fists in frustration at being made to play games to get it back.

"Mr. Lloyd?"

"Yeah, I'm Lloyd," he called down the hall to the fancy man as he started toward him. "What the hell's it to ya' anyway? Some strange son-of-a-bitch outside told me this is where I get my gun back."

"Ah, yes, your gun," the man started as Lloyd's long-gaited steps closed the distance between them. "The exquisitely rare LeMat! What a stunning piece well suited for a talented gunfighter such as yourself."

"What do you know of it, huh?" Lloyd stepped up in the man's face now. "Do you have my gun? Is it you I have to win it from, because if so, I think I like my chances already?"

Lloyd grabbed the man by his shirt and pulled him close, spraying his face with the spit flying out from between his teeth. The man slowly brought his hands up, signifying he wasn't going to act aggressively in return. He didn't flinch and showed not a sign of fear in his eyes. The reaction changed Lloyd's mind and had him thinking the man might actually give him a run for his money. It didn't matter how fancy a man dressed or talked; Lloyd had been doing this long enough to know a stone-cold killer when he looked one in the eyes. He loosened his grip some on the Englishman's shirt but didn't back down, refusing to give up any ground.

"No sir, Lloyd," the man said. "You can relax. I assure you I have no part or hand in any of the games. I'm more of a facilitator of sorts. Would you mind?"

Lloyd lowered his arms and took a reluctant step, maintaining menacing eye contact with the Englishman.

"Right then." The man stuck his hand out to Lloyd. "The name's Bertie, and it's a pleasure to finally meet you, sir."

"The hell kinda' name's 'Bertie'?"

Lloyd did not shake the man's outstretched hand, and Bertie retracted it slowly.

"It's a family name, I'm afraid, but I'm sure you're not

interested in the topic of etymology. Not when there's more pressing matters to attend to."

"Eta—what?"

"Exactly." Bertie clasped his hands in front of him. "Now, let's get to the business of your gun."

Fresh anger washed anew through Lloyd at the mention of his gun, and the little amount of patience he'd been able to conjure was all but gone. He was sick of whatever the hell this foolishness was already.

"Yes, let's," Lloyd managed through clenched teeth.

"Now, I assume you're familiar with the standard fare of your everyday gambling hall games? Your poker, Faro, Keno, Mexican Monte and the like."

Lloyd wasn't much of a gambler, himself being more interested in a sure thing. If he wanted money from someone, he'd flash the LeMat and take it, or shoot them and still take it. He knew of poker and heard stories of professional gamblers winning big at Faro out on the riverboats, but didn't know what the game entailed. He didn't feel like listening to an explanation though, and nodded, gesturing for Bertie to continue.

"It so happens *none* of those games are played here at the Cocytus Gambling Hall. We specialize in a different type of game. One where tremendous risk yields equally sized rewards, but the odds lean heavily toward the favor of the house."

"So, what's that mean?" Lloyd was anxious to get this over with, his voice rising again. "The game is rigged? How am I supposed to win a rigged game?"

"Not rigged exactly, no," answered Bertie. "but not exactly *fair* either. You see, in Cocytus, we don't pretend to have the player's best interest at heart. We're a business after all, and businesses need to take certain measures to stay viable as it were."

Lloyd's head swam with anxious confusion, and it was getting harder to keep his thoughts straight. All the questions he'd pushed to the wayside upon realizing his gun was missing were spinning at a dizzying pace through his mind making it impossible to focus on any one individually. He had to at least know more about his surroundings before going any farther with the farce he'd been sucked into.

"Cocytus? What is this place, anyway? I've done my share of traveling and ain't ever heard of it. Where are the other people? There weren't no one outside but some crazy-talkin' bastard. I don't even know how the hell I got here myself."

"Those are fair and valid questions," Bertie said. "And I will do m—"

"And rules, too." Lloyd cut him off. "Son-of-a-bitch said something about 'the rules' and having to know 'em, only he couldn't tell me what they were."

"As I was saying, Lloyd," continued Bertie. "I will do my absolute best to answer your questions. First off, I don't blame you for never having heard of Cocytus. It's not a place anyone goes looking for to visit and for good reason. You see, our little town has been here for . . . quite some time. The thing is, no one comes here unless they're looking to get something back or something that's been lost to them, and even then, they don't come willingly."

"I didn't lose nothin' but my gun and only because *you* took it from me. I wasn't lookin' for nothin', and I *know* I certainly didn't come here on my own."

Lloyd fought the fog in his head, working to erase the little he remembered about what happened before he arrived in this place. A moment later, he'd forgotten about the Calamity Three coming to Cochran, and how most of the men in town just up and left one day. The image he'd seen of himself so clearly walking behind the general store to sneak up on the bandits went from murky to opaque, and his head hurt the more he probed the darkness for the memory.

"Again, Lloyd, *I* have nothing to do with your gun being taken and suggest you think a little harder about what you may really be looking for."

Lloyd already didn't like the well-groomed Englishman, but the continued use of flowery language and words he didn't understand further nurtured his disdain.

"I ain't been doin' nothin' but thinkin' since I got here, and I'm gettin' pretty sick of riddles."

"Well, you may want to keep that thinking cap dusted off and ready," Bertie said. "You can't find what you're looking for if you don't know what it is."

"Alright, alright," Lloyd said. "You got me here somehow to play your stupid little game and seein' as I ain't got no other choice in the matter. I'll go along with it for now. But you listen here, when that LeMat is back in my hand where it belongs, and it will be sooner than later, the first shot I fire will be in your smarmy fuckin' mouth. When I find out who else is responsible for bringing me to this crazy place, well; I'm gonna' put one between their eyes."

Bertie looked down, frowning, smoothed the front of his suit again, and started to pace.

"And here I was under the impression your new friend outside told you that such acts of aggression will not stand in Cocytus and come with penalties attached that will put you much, *much* farther away from where you need to be."

"Yeah, he told me somethin' of the like," spat Lloyd, "but it don't mean I believe it none."

Bertie stopped pacing and his face went stern and serious. His eyes flashed with the danger Lloyd saw in them earlier that put a twinge of fear in him he didn't like one bit. He hadn't been afraid, truly afraid, in so long he'd forgotten what it felt like. It was colder than he remembered. Lloyd was starting to think he might not get a chance to try his hand at any of these unique games if he continued to put the man off.

If he wanted his gun back, if he wanted to get out of here, if he wanted to live long enough to pull his wife and son from the jaws of a dying town, he was going to have to play ball. It was that simply because he had no other choice. A sharp scraping sound broke his train of thought, and it took him a second to realize Bertie was grinding his teeth. The look on the Englishman's face had gone dark and ghoulish. His nostrils flared dramatically, making each breath an exclamation.

"Fine," Lloyd sighed. "Let's just get on with it. What's the game?"

Bertie's face lit up, the tense hostility of his expression fell away, and his jovial smile returned with a spark of light in the cold dead-spot in his eyes.

"Splendid, Lloyd. Absolutely splendid." He practically sung the words. "Good to see you come around to our way of doing things. I have to admit, you had me worried there for just a moment. As far as the game is concerned, or rather *your* game, it's different for everyone. Like I said, it really is *your* game."

Lloyd tamped down his rising anger, an automatic response to yet another vague string of nonsense. He was done trying to get any real answers out of Bertie.

"Okay, so let's play *my* game already," Lloyd grumbled. "Where do we go?"

"It's actually you not we." Bertie smiled. "I'm afraid I must man my post here. I have another appointment shortly, so you will be on your own for the game. Mostly on your own."

"Appointment? I didn't make no appointment to come here."

Bertie ignored Lloyd, stepped to the side, and gestured to a door behind him. Lloyd didn't remember a door being there, but he hadn't been paying close enough attention, and it didn't matter, anyway.

"Right this way, my friend, right this way."

Bertie smiled again, pausing a moment before reaching for the handle and pulling open the door.

"What in the goddamn hell . . . "

# WRANGLING BLUES

THEY STABLED THE beastly steeds on the backside of Lycus's expansive plot of land before starting the walk up to the large black house on the hill. The Calamity Three had been gone from Cocytus for thirty-one days wrangling up the men Alastor's call couldn't bring in. Of course, they took care of some 'personal business' like killing a cattle rancher and his family for no reason other than it was on the way to their next stop. They set the house and barn on fire and broke open the gate to watch the confused bovine flee the flames by running out into the desert and certain death.

The men were saddle sore and hungry, and not in the mood to deal with Lycus or his mute sidekick, but the three of them would rather get it over with sooner than later. Afterwards, it'd be nothing but uninterrupted sleep, food, whiskey, and whores until they had to go wrangling again. The Three were getting sick of the frequency with which these outings were occurring and planned on letting Lycus know how they felt. Paimon rolled up a smoke as they walked silently across the field.

"Well hell, Paimon, why dontcha' go and roll one of those up for me while you're at it?"

Samuel growled the request, his throat beyond parched from riding the last half of the day with a dry canteen, but it would still be whiskey over water for him tonight.

"'Bout you?" Paimon pointed at Luke, who waved it off, shaking his head.

Paimon rolled the best smokes in all of Texas, which to the three of them was all that mattered. Not only that, but he used a unique tobacco blend Samuel and Luke weren't familiar with. He said it was a family recipe, said his daddy taught him how to make it. When Samuel smoked one of Paimon's rollies, he felt a keenly heightened sense of awareness. He felt sharp. Luke said all it did was make him tired, so he rarely smoked what Paimon rolled up.

Samuel struck a match on his gun handle to light the offering, pulling deeply from the expertly crafted cigarette. He released the smoke slowly through his nostrils, and it hung in the still night air like a specter.

"How come there ain't ever no goddamn wind in this place? Not even a breeze."

Samuel asked this all the time, and neither Luke nor Paimon had an answer for him.

"How come Lycus's little bitch can't get 'em all with her. .. whatever the hell it is she does with her brain?" Now Luke started on one of his rants. "And why the hell does Lycus need the ones she can't bring in so bad that we gotta go out and get the bastards?"

"I guess that's the question we all want to know the answer to." Paimon spoke slowly but clearly, despite his drawl.

None of them brought up the one man they didn't bring back with them, but he'd just up and vanished as far any of them could tell. Didn't make sense to waste time on him.

"Well, I say we aim to find out tonight," huffed Luke, quickening his pace.

Samuel sighed, wishing Luke would've taken Paimon up on the smoke before he went and got himself all worked up. They were almost up the hill now and could see Alastor standing by the backdoor staring a hole down into the Calamity Three. Her eyes flashed purple in the full moon's light, but the moon was always full in Cocytus.

"I hate that creepy bastard," Samuel whispered to Paimon.

He didn't lower his voice because he was afraid. He was honestly just too tired to start anything with her. The door was open behind her and the smell of cooked meat wafted out coaxing the men to hurry along convincing them they could wait until their bellies were full to list their grievances to Lycus. Samuel and Paimon caught up to Luke, and Alastor moved to the side as the men entered.

Luke ignored the girl and Samuel snarled while Paimon tipped his hat and offered a ma'am as they filed past before she stepped in behind them pulling the door closed. There was a dining room in the house, but they entered through the kitchen, surprised to find Lycus sitting at the smaller table there waiting for them. The food the men smelled was piled high across the table, and Lycus was already cutting into a piece of ham from the plate in front of him.

"Gentlemen," Lycus said, pausing to take a bite. "Welcome back. Sit. Eat."

The Calamity Three sauntered to the table and sat hard on the empty chairs, waiting for them. Samuel spotted and snatched a bottle of whiskey at the center of the table, tore the cork out with his teeth, and drank deeply before passing it to Luke who did the same before handing it off to Paimon. The bottle was empty after the first go around and surreptitiously replaced by Alastor who stood behind Lycus hovering in his periphery as always.

"More where that came from," Lycus said through another bite of ham. "Plenty more."

The men loaded their plates with meat, bread, and potatoes without speaking. They ate like starved coyotes gone mad with hunger, swallowing whole mouthfuls without chewing. Lycus smiled and watched while eating at a much slower, more civilized pace. His long silver hair was pulled back behind his shoulders, and his accompanying sideburns had been recently trimmed and made less unruly. Lycus's house reflected a taste for certain fineries, but he still dressed like he was riding the trail.

You'd expect a man like him to wear something fancier, being he hadn't left Cocytus for as long as the Calamity Three had been working with him.

Another bottle of whiskey went around, and mounds of food were devoured before the men showed any sign of slowing, and even then, it took a third bottle to stop them completely. Paimon rolled a smoke as the sounds of consumption died down to the low murmuring of stomachs digesting a week's worth of meals at one time.

"So," Lycus smiled. "All full?"

"We're sick of this wrangling horse shit," Luke said without missing a beat.

"We don't wanna go on no more of these hunts of yours unless you *really* make it worth our while," Samuel added on the heels of his partner while picking his teeth.

Paimon smoked and nodded.

"I'm confused," Lycus's tone was goading. "Do I not make it worth your while already?"

He gestured to the scraps of what had been enough food to feed ten men, his eyebrows raised.

"Goddamnit!" Luke pounded the table with a meaty fist. "Now, listen—"

"No, you listen." Lycus cut the man off. His tone went deep and cold, stripped of playful humor. "You three are in *no* position to make demands of *me*, or do you forget our arrangement?"

Samuel felt his hand involuntarily move to his gun but stopped when Alastor stepped up. The three men remembered the 'agreement'; they just didn't care.

"You boys missed one." Lycus was speaking of the man in Cochran who vanished on them. "And on top of that you come back and make demands of me?"

"Weren't our fault! He disappeared," Samuel fired back.

"What difference does it make, anyway?" Luke added. "Why don't you just have wonder-girl there use her fancy brainpowers to get him iffin' he means so much to ya'?"

Lycus rose, threw the table to the side, and pulled Luke from his chair by his shirt.

"That's exactly what I did, you halfwit pig-fucker! And the three of you should be thanking Alastor for getting him here when you couldn't, because if not for that we wouldn't be having this conversation right now."

He dropped Luke in his chair and stepped back with Alastor right beside him, bandana pulled tight across the lower half of her face. At first, they'd thought she couldn't talk because she didn't have a lower jaw until they saw her eat one time she went wrangling with them. They didn't know why she always wore it, and they didn't care.

"So, are you sayin' you got him? The guy what vanished on us is here?" Luke asked.

"That's what I'm *sayin'*," Lycus's tone was once again laced with venomous wit but maintained a terrifyingly authoritative quality. "No thanks to you."

The three men watched Lycus turn to leave the kitchen, but he paused at the door and faced them again. The smile had returned to his face.

"Gentlemen, you know where the whiskey and women are, and if you find yourself still hungry, there's a whole other spread laid out for you in the dining room. Get some rest boys. We still have work to do."

He left without giving them a chance to respond and Alastor followed close behind. The Calamity Three sat staring at the empty doorway while Paimon rolled another smoke.

"Goddamnit," Samuel said. "I forgot to ask why there ain't no goddamn wind."

# TO TOWN WE ARE A GOIN'

THE LAST TIME Cherub's mother came to the house was on his tenth birthday, but not because she'd planned it that way. Emma was barely aware of her son's existence, the notion becoming a foggy memory locked away in a part of her brain she'd since been denied access. All other information pertaining to Cherub and eventually even Lloyd had been wiped clean, including birthdays. Her stumbling into the house that particular day was nothing but coincidence.

Cherub stayed in his room, the Colt beneath his mattress, and waited until she'd left again. He didn't feel much like celebrating, not with her, at least. He'd never held a grudge toward his mother regarding her failings and was still sympathetic when it came to her addiction. He didn't blame Emma for what the morphine did to her, but after a while he started to blame her for letting it take over, for not trying harder to get away from it and clean up. Cherub loved his mother dearly, but the resentment started once it became clear he'd been replaced completely by the drug.

She cared for, coddled, and nurtured her addiction while Cherub was left without his mother's, albeit misdirected, love and guidance. It'd gotten to the point he started hoping she'd move into the hotel permanently where she could trade pokes for poison until she was nothing but a numbed-out brain in a jar attached to a warm wet hole. He was too young to be hardened in such a way, but some kids are made to grow up fast. He had no choice.

He found a potato sack she'd left on the table with a loaf of bread and half a wheel of cheese inside, although she'd taken the two plates and only set of silverware in the house. He didn't figure she meant to leave the sack having more than likely forgotten she'd put it down until she was all the way back at the hotel beneath a sweaty, panting cowboy pumping away.

He ate the bread and cheese slowly over several days having learned to ration any food his mother brought home since he never knew when she'd be back or what she may bring. The food ran out without her returning first, and after going three full days without eating a thing, Cherub decided he needed to do something. He'd never been away from the property on his own and had only been to town a handful of times with his mother, but he remembered which direction it was in and started walking.

The belt the holster for the Peacemaker was attached to was far too big for him, but he made it work by wrapping it twice around his slender waist. The Colt was loaded with the last five bullets left, which was another reason for making the trip. He needed food and cartridges, and if he found his mother, that would be a good thing too, but it wasn't a priority.

While Cherub knew what direction town was in, he didn't know much else and wracked his brain trying to remember details wishing he'd paid more attention the few times he'd been out. He resigned himself to continue the way he was going, knowing he'd eventually run into town or someone who'd be able to put him on the right track.

After about an hour of walking his empty belly started to grumble and cramp, and he pulled the doubled-up gun belt another notch tighter to cinch away his hunger pains. The sun was high and hot, working to sap what little strength he had, and the gun hanging from his hip got heavier with each step. No matter how much his body begged him to stop, Cherub refused and pressed on in spite of his pain and exhaustion.

He thought he was hallucinating and didn't register the sound of a horse approaching from the rear was real until it was nearly on top of him. Cherub reeled, trying to spin on his heel while drawing the Colt, but instead tripped over his own feet and fell forward, landing on his chin with the gun still in the holster. This wasn't the way he envisioned starting his career as a gunfighter, which was in danger of being over before it begun. The horse stopped, and the rider dismounted as Cherub lifted his head. He expected to see the barrel of a gun for a moment, then nothing else ever again, but instead there was a hand.

He looked up at a face he was familiar with but did not personally know and reached out to accept the hand that pulled him to his feet. It was more the horse Cherub recognized, as he'd seen it pass by the property going to and from town countless times. The mare had a dazzling burgundy colored coat speckled with white spots that appeared to sparkle in the sun. Its mane and tail were bright blonde, and Cherub thought they looked like fiery white flames when the horse ran at a full gallop. He'd been so enamored with the animal he never paid close attention to its rider, this being the longest he'd looked at them, and while he hadn't expected it to be a woman, he wasn't surprised or put off.

He'd been raised by his mother and was around her almost exclusively his entire life so far, and having not been introduced to what society deemed appropriate roles based on gender, he remained unaffected. Their bond may have become strained or even close to severed at this point, but as far as he was concerned, a woman could do just as much as any man. He'd seen his mother do it with his own eyes day after day before her troubles started.

"Whatcha' doin' out her alone, boy?" The woman asked, looking down at him. "You don't even have on a hat."

Cherub ran his hand through his sweaty hair, realizing for the first time he'd foolishly left home without it. The woman wasn't old, but the better part of her youth was behind her. He guessed she could be around the same age as his mother, but appeared years younger; her features untouched by the debilitating effects of the demon morphine. Her strawberry curls were pinned back so her hat would stay low and titled forward to keep the sun from touching her face. No amount of shade was able to dull the bright green of her eyes, though. Their gleam seemed able to cleave through even the darkest shadows.

Before Cherub could say anything, the woman pulled a canteen from her saddlebag and handed it to him, though he stood silent, hesitant to accept the offer.

"Just take a drink. I know you're thirsty," she said. "Don't be scared. In fact, if anything, it should be *me* who's scared, what with you being the one with the gun."

His gun. He'd tripped over himself trying to draw the thing, then forgot all about the hunk of iron hanging awkwardly from his side.

"Oh, I . . . I mean, I'm—"

"I know who you are," she said, placing the canteen in his hand forcing him to take it. "I mean, I don't know your name or nothin', but I seen you when I ride past. You live in the house on that property, back down the road a piece, right?"

Cherub nodded before removing the lid to drink greedily from the canteen.

"I live about three miles down from you," she continued, now pulling a handkerchief from her back pocket to hand the boy. "Name's Caroline."

"I'm Cha . . . Cherub."

He took his lips away from the canteen before using the handkerchief to wipe his face. He could feel the coarse dust and grime mix with his sweat as he ran the cloth down his cheeks. No hat, no water, filthy and already taken by surprise. Some gunfighter he was shaping up to be.

"Nice meetin' you, Cherub. Now, do you want to tell me what you're doing so far from your house with nothin' but a gun the size of your leg strapped to you?"

Something in his brain shook loose allowing the wheels to turn again, and Cherub composed himself ignoring the embarrassment over being ill-prepared for his trip. He honestly thought he'd have been in town by now, maybe even already on the way back. He had little grasp over distance and time though and was currently finding out the hard way.

"I'm headin' into town for some supplies, ma'am," Cherub said. "I'm pleased to meet ya, Miss Caroline, and I surely do appreciate the water."

He handed the canteen back to Caroline, and she narrowed her eyes upon taking it back.

"I reckon I'm doing the same myself." The woman drank deeply from the canteen before returning it to the saddlebag. "Why is it you're going alone and on foot at that? It's a pretty far walk, and how were you plannin' to bring back these supplies you're after with no cart, or horse, or even a sack to carry?"

He swallowed hard. "I reckon I'll manage."

Cherub looked down the trail ahead, having no idea how much further it was to town.

"And your mother? What of her?"

Caroline's eyes flashed like emeralds beneath the brim of her hat, and he found it difficult to look away.

"She's . . . I'm going by myself. I am the man of the house."

Cherub thought the words sounded better in his head, but they came out weak, lacking conviction. He wasn't quite sure what to say after that, so he nodded to Miss Caroline and started walking down the trail again. He stuck close to the side this time to allow plenty of room for the woman and her horse to pass. Cherub snuck a look over his shoulder after walking ten feet without hearing her approach and saw she was still standing next to the gorgeous mare staring down the trail at him. He could see she was smiling.

"Cherub," she called out. "I had a thought. Seein' as we're both going to town, and we're both alone. Maybe you could ride in with me. It never hurts to have another set of eyes out here, and I don't figure we'll have much trouble once they see that Colt you're carrying."

Cherub stopped and turned around. He didn't want to accept any help. He wanted to do this on his own; he wanted to prove to himself he could. He was decidedly out of his depth though, and unprepared to go it alone. This time. He decided he'd take her up on the offer of the ride, but only so he could better learn the way for the next time he went to town. He doubted he'd even need a ride back home. Cherub shrugged and walked back down the path to Caroline.

"Seein' as you need some protection," he said. "I reckon I'll take the rest of the ride into town with you."

"I appreciate the favor. Let me help you into the saddle."

He was close enough now her smile was almost blinding, and she bent to help push him up after he managed to lift his leg high enough to put his foot in the stirrup. It happened when she put both hands on the boy. That was when she saw it.

Caroline was gifted in certain ways most people would say classified her as a witch, and they wouldn't be wrong. She lived on the far outskirts of town alone and kept to herself so as not to rouse any suspicion. Caroline didn't draw upon the darkness for power as some witches did, but it didn't matter in the eyes of any good, god-fearing person. To them, all witches were the same, and they were all evil.

Caroline communed with the earth and drew from the natural energies around her to practice her craft, but it was her inborn ability that allowed her to do so. She'd had visions in the past, not with much regularity though, and she never saw anything of real consequence. It was mostly weather patterns and other natural occurrences that helped her manage the garden she kept. She sustained herself primarily on food she grew and used the herbs for various spells and the occasional elixir. Sometimes she'd see a flash of something she'd thought was lost and know exactly where it was. What Caroline saw when she lifted Cherub into the saddle was neither trivial nor banal.

The images flashing through her mind in that fraction of a second were vivid portrayals of violence, betrayal, suffering, and death. The overbearing wretchedness of which caused her breath to hitch and put a lump in her throat. Worst of all, there was nothing she could do to stop it.

# NO ONE COMES BACK THROUGH

**BERTIE KNOCKED TWICE** sharply on the front door and let himself in. Usually, the Englishman was more polite than to do so, but Lycus was expecting him. It didn't excuse his behavior in his mind, but was at least slightly less offensive. Lycus sat in a chair upholstered for comfort next to the fireplace, picking his teeth while Alastor used a poker to stoke the flames.

Bertie smoothed his hair and twisted the ends of his mustache as he approached and took the empty seat across from his employer. It was solid wood and not nearly as comfortable. Alastor leaned the poker against the wall and stood next to Lycus, her purple eyes staring a hate-hole through the Englishman. He'd gotten too far down a whiskey bottle one night a month back and let his hands wander where they were most certainly not wanted.

She'd made him pay for it, and his hand was in fact still healing, but she would *not* let him forget. Now Bertie was incredibly uncomfortable around Alastor feeling like he was always a pussy-hair away from a beat-down. If he had any idea how powerful she was, what she could *really* do to him, he'd know better than to ever come around her again.

"You're late," Lycus started.

"Yes, well, I do apologize. It took a little longer than expected to get him to . . . join the game."

Lycus didn't reply right away, and a silence hung between them, further stalling the already stilted dialogue.

"But he is . . . in?" He finally asked.

"Yes, sir, he is. I saw him in myself and shut the door behind him." Bertie nodded like his head was on a spring.

"Startin' to lose your touch Bertie-Boy." Lycus smiled. "Thought I was gonna' have to come throw him in myself."

Bertie hated the nickname his boss had given him, but was in no position to protest. He was only in Cocytus because Lycus pulled him out of his eternal suffering in the void and put him to work. He'd already pressed his luck with the Alastor incident and was deathly afraid of being cast back in the darkness to which he'd been formerly relegated. It wasn't worth defending himself over.

"Well . . . I. . . . yes, I suppose I could've negotiated the situation better, faster. I do appreciate the help, though."

It was Lycus who'd been the 'cowboy stranger' from the saloon Lloyd talked to outside the gambling hall. This wasn't typical behavior, seeing as he didn't feel the need to involve himself directly in the culling process, but this was too important. The Calamity Three nearly mucked up the whole thing by not being able to wrangle Lloyd, and Lycus was lucky Alastor grabbed him when she did. It was proof the girl was getting stronger just like he knew she would. Usually, a newcomer to Cocytus would wander the street for a bit before eventually finding their way into the gambling hall where Bertie took over, but he couldn't take any more risks.

He needed Lloyd to play the game, and now he had him doing just that. The hard part was over, and it was time to wait. What lie at the end of Lloyd's game would make him a valuable ally, or it would make him dead with Lycus benefitting from either outcome.

"It's good to know a man like you is open to criticism and self-improvement. I'd say that's a good trait to have, wouldn't you, Alastor?"

Alastor, of course, said nothing, but Bertie felt the

intensity of the gaze she aimed at him ratchet up several notches. It was making his face hot.

"So, what's next on the agenda?" Bertie tried to steer the subject away from the impromptu performance critique. "I mean, what can I do for you next? Did I hear Calamity was back in town as well?"

"Yep. Just missed 'em."

Lycus pulled a thin cigar from his shirt pocket, smiled, and reached out offering it to Bertie.

"Oh, uh, no thank you."

Bertie cleared his throat. Refusing when one is offered something was another act he considered rude, inexcusably so for the most part, but he'd smoked one of Lycus's cigars before. It was a most unpleasant experience, and rather than tempt fate in thinking it could've been an isolated incident, it was better to forsake his manners and decline. Bertie didn't know what was in them, but it was like no tobacco he'd ever smoked and made his lungs feel like they'd been scraped raw with broken glass. The pain lasted for weeks after.

"Suit yourself."

Lycus put the cigar to his mouth and Alastor touched a lit match to the end as he puffed it to life. She moved so fast Bertie wasn't entirely sure the girl had even struck a match and not produced fire from thin air. He rolled the cigar between his thumb and finger while smoke slowly escaped his mouth and curled up the side of his face momentarily obscuring the sinister grin leveled at Bertie. Lycus took another deep pull before speaking again.

"No Bertie, I reckon there ain't no more I need from you, at least for the moment. You can head back on down to the gambling hall and make sure you keep that door closed. You hear me? Nothin', and I mean *nothin'*, comes back through or being returned to eternal darkness and torture will be a welcome alternative to what *I* do to you."

The Englishman was confused but too scared to ask for an explanation. Nothing and no one had ever come back through the door once Bertie shut it behind them. As far as he'd known, once someone entered the game, that was it. There was no coming back once the 'choice' had been forced upon them. Their souls added weight to Cocytus, the kind of weight Lycus needed to rip through time and release Behemoth so the mammoth tyrant could drag the other side through with him. He'd never allow them to escape once they were already in town, although he may string them along, let them to believe the possibility of freedom was real.

"Yes sir. Very good," Bertie finally managed as he stood hesitating before continuing. "Is there . . . what I mean is, do you think this Lloyd may be able to come back through? Does he truly have the ability to do so?"

The smile fell from Lycus, and he stood towering over Bertie by a foot and a half.

"If he does have the ability to come back through, you'll never know, because that's how fast I'll snap your limey pencil neck if it happens. How about that? Keep. The. Door. Closed."

"Very good, sir," Bertie dropped his head. "Very good."

He skulked away keeping his eyes to the floor until he reached the door and was back outside. Bertie walked down the path away from the house as Lycus's booming laughter carried across the windless Cocytus night.

"Tell Magoth to take care of him," Lycus said to Alastor when he'd stopped laughing. "He asks too many stupid questions."

# LET THE GAME BEGIN

**LLOYD STEPPED SLOWLY** through the door the Englishman opened for him and found himself back outside on the street he'd just left only now the town was bustling with activity. He heard the door slam and wheeled around to find only a wall behind him. Lloyd reached out and ran his hand across the wood feeling for the hidden seams of a door, but there were none. He stepped back and examined the wall, turned his neck, and leaned from one side to the other hoping the light would catch just right to reveal the concealed door, but it just wasn't there.

"The hell . . . " Lloyd muttered turning back to face the scene around him.

It was the same street alright. He recognized the saloon where the stranger had been standing only now it was full of people and alive with energy, the swinging doors in constant motion from their comings and goings. Fifty feet down the way to his right was where he'd entered the gambling hall.

There hadn't been a single soul on the street save for the smoking cowboy, but now suddenly there wasn't anywhere he could look without seeing people. It took a moment for Lloyd to register what was happening before it all became clear. There was a fair going on, and the groups of people were crowded around carnival games either participating or watching while whooping and hollering in collective joy or despair. There were couples walking arm in arm on their way from one game to another or coming and going from the saloon.

Lloyd pushed his confoundedness aside to focus on what he was here to do, get back his gun and make whoever'd taken it realize it was the worst and last mistake they'd ever make. He looked up and down the street one more time before crossing on his way to the saloon. He figured someone amongst the gathered crowd would be able to point him in the direction of whatever game he was supposed to play, or know someone who could. He was about to put his boot on the sidewalk in front of the saloon when he was given the answer.

"Oh, Lloyd."

The call came from behind and he spun out of instinct grabbing for a gun that wasn't there.

"Lloyd, I'm afraid it's not time for the saloon just yet, at least not for you. You see, you need to have a reason to celebrate, and you've yet to earn the privilege, I'm afraid."

The man was a dwarf of less than four feet with short black hair dramatically parted in the center and slicked down against his scalp. He wore red-striped pants held up by suspenders over a dingy shirt with a sweat-wilted collar. His gap-toothed smile was too wide for his face and seemed to get bigger as he approached.

"That one of these rules I've been hearin' so much about?" Lloyd said.

"As a matter of fact, it is," the man said extending his hand. "The name's Magoth. It's truly a pleasure to make your acquaintance."

"Ain't no one here with a normal name?" Lloyd grumbled and reached down to shake the man's hand. "The weird bastard inside said I gotta play some specific game to get my gun back. You know where I can find it?"

"Yes, sir, that is exactly why I'm here."

The small man's smile stretched to his ears now, and the warped sight of it made Lloyd's stomach tumble.

"Well, spit it out Mag—Maggot."

"Magoth," he corrected. "And of course, of course. You're anxious to play, I'm sure, and I'm here to assist. Please, follow me."

Magoth hooked his thumbs in his suspenders and walked past Lloyd toward the alley running between the saloon and the Cocytus Gambling Hall across the street from the one he'd gone into. He wondered for a moment if the outcome would've been the same had he gone there instead, but it didn't matter now. Lloyd watched warily, unsure if he was supposed to go with him, or if he even wanted to. The man stopped just before disappearing between the buildings and gestured with an emphatic wave for him to follow and, having no other choice; he did.

He stepped into the alley, and Magoth was already at the other end still smiling while waving him on with both hands now. The backside of the building looked well-lit from where Lloyd was standing, which made him feel a little better about following the stranger, but he wouldn't be completely at ease until he had his LeMat. For that, he needed to play the game and follow the rules, but then all bets were off. Lloyd stepped quicker down the alley eager to get on with it.

Magoth had gone behind the saloon and was out of sight when Lloyd made the corner trying to catch up. He stopped dead in his tracks when he saw it and would've smiled had the circumstances been different. Sprawled out across the open land behind the buildings was a shooting range, albeit on the extravagant side, but Lloyd knew a range when he saw one. If this was the game they wanted him to play, he'd have his gun back in no time.

"I take it you like what you see?"

Lloyd couldn't tell where the voice was coming from at first, surprised to find Magoth was closer than he thought. The small man was just off to the left standing next to a small round table covered with a red cloth. He had both arms raised in presentation of the range; the lower half of his face still smeared in an exaggerated smile.

"If it's what I think it is, I reckon I like it just fine," Lloyd said walking over to the table.

"You're a smart man, Lloyd" Magoth looked up at him. "You know a turnip farm when you see one."

"What?" Lloyd narrowed his eyes confused and looked back down the range. "A turnip . . . what?"

Magoth coughed out a short halting burst of high-pitched laughter and slapped the tabletop.

"Of course, it's a gun range. I'm only pulling your leg. You should lighten up some Lloyd, things aren't so bad. Yet."

Lloyd ignored the man's laughter along with the last comment he'd made and took a good long look down the range. It appeared to be set up in stages, one after another, spanning on for over a hundred yards with no discernable end in sight. A tall sign stood at the start of each stage displaying a whimsical painting of a different gun.

The first sign directly in front of him quite clearly displayed a generic Derringer but showed no identifiable markings to indicate manufacturer. Lloyd looked back down at Magoth, who, as if on cue, pulled the red cloth from the table revealing a tiny gun beneath. Lloyd could tell right off it was a Remington model Deringer, single barrel, one shot. He'd never been a Remington man himself, but brand name had no bearing on his talent. If it had a trigger, he could shoot it and shoot it well.

"Each station along the range is marked with the specific type of gun you are to use to play that particular part of the game," continued Magoth. "The number of shots you're permitted to take varies depending on the gun and how far along in the game you get."

"So, I take it I gotta use that there Derringer here at the start?"

"That is correct!"

"And I imagine since it only holds one bullet, that's all I get for this first . . . challenge or whatever the hell you called it?"

"Right again! Lloyd, I have a good feeling about you, and I don't have good feelings about anybody."

Magoth was beaming up at Lloyd who could almost see his reflection in the shine of the man's hair.

"Is that supposed to make me feel better? 'Cause it don't."

The smile dropped from Magoth's face for the first time since their encounter began. Its absence affected the rest of his features as they arranged themselves into an unpleasant sneer. The sudden juxtaposition was jarring as he took on a monstrous appearance hardly resembling who he was moments ago.

"Lloyd." Magoth's voice went low and scratchy, his tone ice-cold. "I don't give a shit about you or your feelings. You're no more than a braindead heap of trash to me, which I will take great pleasure in incinerating. This game is only prolonging the inevitable."

He punctuated the statement with a hiss that hung in the windless air between them until the smile snapped back into place as suddenly as it had gone.

"Now, I know you're anxious, so let's get started." Magoth clapped his small chubby hands together then gestured once again to the Derringer, the enthusiastic high-pitched whine returned to his voice. "As you guessed, you have one shot with this Derringer to hit a moving target."

Lloyd reached out and took the gun from the table. It was small and light, but he felt good having a gun his hand, and his confidence increased exponentially in that moment. He was born to shoot, and any doubt trying to creep into his mind evaporated. He checked the barrel, ensured it was loaded, then turned it over in his hand for a quick general inspection.

"So, where's the target? Ain't nothin' movin' out there."

He looked down and Magoth pointed at the large wooden switch built into the sidewalk next to the table. He pulled it to the side and Lloyd detected motion from down the range in his peripheral. He looked out and saw a wooden target shaped like the silhouette of a chicken attached to a thin rail.

The other end was attached to some kind of small track in the dirt, but Lloyd couldn't tell exactly how it worked from where he stood. The chicken facsimile was about chest high and moved six feet back and forth with virtually no pause when changing direction, but it was the distance not the movement that was troubling.

The target was a minimum of fifty feet out, which is twice the distance a Derringer can shoot. It doesn't matter who manufactures the thing. They're made to be used at close range, and the closer the better because even a pointblank shot isn't guaranteed to kill a man.

"The hell's this supposed to be?" Lloyd gestured out at the wooden chicken.

"It's the moving target. The one you're to hit if you want to move on in the game, with one shot, of course."

Lloyd watched the chicken move side to side a few more times, shook his head, and stared down the small squirrely man.

"You know, same as me, that target is out of range for a gun like this. It's at least twice as far away as this thing can shoot on a good day. How the hell am I supposed to hit something that far away whether it moves or not?"

"I'm afraid I can only tell you how to play the game, not how to win. Where would the fun in that be? It wouldn't be much of a game if you ask me?"

Lloyd bit back his rage, but it was getting harder to control. He remembered what the Englishman in the gambling hall told him how the games favored the house with no compunction, but this was more than just *favor,* it was a sure thing.

"Not much of a game?" Lloyd pointed down the range. "This ain't no game at all. It's a goddamn impossibility is what it is!"

Magoth smiled up at the frustrated gunfighter and

shrugged as if to indicate it wasn't his problem. It was Lloyd's turn to sneer now, and he pointed the Derringer down holding it inches from the man's face.

"And what's stoppin' me from puttin' this one bullet in your head? Supposin' I do that then tear this game, or whatever you call it, apart until I find my LeMat and shoot your corpse again on the way out."

"Nothing is stopping you from doing anything." Magoth was unaffected by the gun in his face. "Of course, shooting me isn't part of the game, and doing so will disqualify you immediately. Retrieving your precious gun in the aftermath would be impossible, though, as you need me to take you to it. Simply destroying the game, much like a child who flips the checkers board in frustration when losing, will not get you any closer to your LeMat. If you want it back, you have to *win* it back. Destruction does not equate victory."

Lloyd went to reply but had nothing to say, nothing that would help the situation. He looked from Magoth to the target and back still debating whether or not to shoot the man. Lloyd figured even if he aced the entire game there was still a good chance he wouldn't get his gun back, and while killing Magoth might disqualify him, it would feel good to do it.

He wracked his brain for every memory he had of shooting a Derringer, but there weren't many. He'd taken one from a man who'd pointed it at him during an argument in a small Texas desert-town saloon. He couldn't recall what the argument was over, only that the man pulled the small gun from inside his jacket, and Lloyd snatched it the instant he saw the glint off the barrel. He flipped the petite pistol around in his hand and shot the man in the thigh before pushing him off the stool and stepping on his chest as he walked out. He liked the idea of a surprise attack and kept the gun strapped to his wrist for a few weeks. He quickly tired of carrying it around though and abandoned the weapon.

Lloyd suddenly recalled something that may help, although it didn't involve him or a Derringer. Clancy, one of the men he used to meet up to do jobs with, got to arguing with a local man in one of the towns they were passing through. He didn't remember what that fight was over either, but when Clancy pulled his Colt, someone ran out of the mercantile shop on his right. The intervening man tackled Clancy forcing his arm up just as he pulled the trigger, and he fired into the air.

The two of them hit the ground and started squabbling right away while the man Clancy had been aiming for ran up to join the fray. Lloyd drew on the pile from atop his horse but couldn't take a shot without risking hitting Clancy, which wouldn't be the worst thing to happen and therefore not out of the question. He decided to close his eyes and shoot when a shrill shriek ripped up the street grabbing all four men's attention followed by frantic pleas for help.

People came out of the buildings to see what was going on, and the two men stopped wrestling with Clancy, detangled themselves, and stood in reaction to the commotion. At the opposite end of the street in front of an old wooden church there was a crowd gathering, and the two men who'd been fighting with Clancy took off running in the direction. He had a clear shot at them and for a few paces could've killed them both with one bullet, but something about the screaming gave him pause. It was full of pain. Deep helpless pain, the kind that never fully goes away. Pain that lasts a lifetime. Clancy felt it as well and scrambled to his feet to see what was happening.

"Go check it out," Clancy called to Lloyd. "I'll get my horse and meet you down there."

Lloyd nodded and headed toward the church at a slow trot. The crowd of people were gathered around something on the ground and Lloyd couldn't see what it was until he rode right up on them. Not a one looked up to acknowledge his approach, and he soon saw why. The source of the screaming was a young woman on her knees at the center of them with soft blonde curls and huge brown bawling eyes. Her face and dress were covered in blood, though none of it her own.

Cradled against her chest was a young boy no older than five bleeding from a hole in his head, and from his vantage point Lloyd could see the light had already left the boys half-open eyes. His mouth hung slack, and a stream of red ran from the side in thin wet threads. Lloyd instantly knew exactly what happened. The woman wailed from a place of inconsolable sadness she would never recover from. He dug his heels into the sides of his horse, pulled the reins, and galloped back toward the approaching Clancy.

He and his horse blew past without slowing and were in fact gaining speed as his confused partner realized too late he should've turned around as well. Lloyd continued to ride away from the town without looking back despite hearing gunfire and what were unmistakably Clancy's screams.

The bullet from the shot gone wild went up as far as it could. It came down much faster and much further down the road, striking the side of the young boy's head, killing him instantly. It was an accidental and senseless death, but one Clancy paid for with his life at the hands of the townsfolk's immediate and deadly retaliation. Lloyd wasn't happy about what happened to the boy, but he wasn't upset about getting rid of Clancy. It meant a bigger slice of the pie for him. Lloyd hadn't thought of the man since the day it all happened years ago, but was glad for the memory to have been jogged.

Lloyd pointed the Derringer away from Magoth and down the range in the direction of the moving wooden chicken. He raised his arm up at roughly a forty-five-degree angle and pulled the trigger. A moment-and-a-half later, the wooden chick exploded into splinters and fell backwards off the track. He dropped the gun in the dirt and turned back to Magoth. The small man's cheerful expression had once again gone missing. It was Lloyd's turn to smile now.

# SLEEPING IT OFF

**SAMUEL AND PAIMON** were sleeping and had been for close to fifteen hours, but Luke remained awake and brooding. The three bandits each had their own room on the second floor of Lycus's home, but they'd passed out in the billiard room down the hall, which also was relegated to only them. They were on the floor in a heap of blankets, one of them drug in from a nearby bedroom. Two naked women flanked both men and were also sleeping soundly.

Paimon preferred the more buxom-type, and his skinny pale frame was a sight squeezed between the thickness of the women, their chests rising and falling in unison. For such a small skinny man, he had a tremendously sized member, which was freakish to Luke even when flaccid. Samuel was naked save for his boots and slept with his hands behind his head while the other two ladies nuzzled against his ample chest. He was still smiling, despite being fast asleep.

There'd been six women in all when the evening started, but Luke sent two of them away, choosing the bottle over a good double-poke. Their dinner conversation with Lycus left him fuming further as he felt no resolution had been reached not to mention how they'd been disrespected, although he wasn't sure how his partners took it. They seemed content to eat a shit sandwich and smile while doing it as long as Lycus kept them rich, drunk, and laid. It was different for Luke though, for him it went deeper than carnality or material wealth could remedy. For Luke, it was personal.

The Calamity Three did their share of carousing and alcohol had blurred if not completely destroyed a good deal of their memories, but there was something about their arrival in Cocytus that left Luke unsettled. There'd been a celebration on the night they met and made a deal to work with Lycus, and the man pulled out all the stops for the bandits. Their whiskey glasses remained perpetually full and thus began the three's ritual of gorging on the food, liquor, and women they now expected upon returning from a wrangle.

What bothered Luke the most was his inability to recall exactly how the Calamity Three came to be in the strange dark town. The men rarely talked about it, but when they had Samuel said something about remembering a sandstorm kicking up out of nowhere, and they'd gotten turned around. When it started to die down, he said he could see something through the dust clouds a hundred or so yards away, so they all rode toward what they discovered was Cocytus. Samuel described it confidently like it was engrained in his memory, but Luke wasn't so sure.

When Samuel went off to the jakes, Luke asked Paimon if he remembered it the same way. He'd said it sounded right but had just as hard a time as Luke trying to draw the memory out from the haze in his mind, and it remained obscured. He remembered getting lost in a sandstorm, but thought it had happened before they'd come to Cocytus. When Luke thought about it, he could recall a time they did get lost in a sandstorm like Samuel said, but it was when they'd been coming up out of Waco a year or so ago. When the dust settled, it wasn't Cocytus they happened upon; it was Killeen.

The three were riled and angry at being lost in the storm and took their frustrations out on the town. They'd stormed the First Bank of Killeen without hesitation and first thing through the door Samuel shot a man in the back standing at the counter talking to a banker. When he fell Samuel fired off another shot into the banker's forehead sending him face first down onto the counter with a wet slap before tumbling back to the floor. The bank smelled like gun smoke and fear, and the Calamity Three fed greedily off the combination they'd come to savor.

Within a matter of minutes, they turned the bank into a bloodbath having killed everyone inside along with the Sheriff and a deputy who came running in upon hearing the shots. The lawmen were in mid-draw when Paimon and Luke gunned them down. Then, the three bandits set the bank on fire without even taking any of the money and rode out of town. Samuel shot a woman in the face who peaked out a window as the men rode by.

Luke was dead certain they hadn't arrived in Cocytus by losing their way in a sandstorm, but for the life of him couldn't remember exactly how. The harder he thought about it, the harder it became to recall, like the memory was being continuously pushed back deeper behind the veil. Not being able to remember made Luke angry, and when he was angry, he drank, which was why he was imbibing so heavily this night as he watched his partners sleep. He didn't like Lycus one bit, never had. He trusted the man even less. He decided right then and there, he was done. Done with wrangling, done with Lycus, done with Cocytus, and if Samuel and Paimon disagreed, he'd be done with them too, though he couldn't imagine they would.

He wasn't content to just pick up and leave in the night like a coward either, Luke aimed to show Lycus and the town of Cocytus what happens when you disrespect the Calamity Three.

Luke tilted his head back, emptying the last of the bottle down his throat, and sensed someone behind him. He swung around in his chair awkwardly, feeling tipsier than anticipated but still too sharp to get the drop on. Alastor was standing in the darkness of the hall just outside the door. Her purple eyes gleamed in a glint of moonlight coming through the window, and she stared the bandit down coldly, knowingly, like she was reading his thoughts aware of his plan as it formulated.

Luke locked eyes with the girl, refusing to be intimidated, waiting for the sentiment to sink in before finally addressing her.

"Well?" Luke growled from his chair. "The hell you want?"

He knew she wouldn't answer, couldn't answer, but still spoke like he expected her to. He didn't like Alastor, but not for the same reasons he didn't like Lycus. She was far more powerful than the three men put together, but he refused to be scared. Nothing and no one was intimidating to Luke, and he'd stared down enemies more imposing than Alastor. He didn't care if she had powers he didn't understand. It would take more than a small-framed mute girl to take him out.

A grunt came from the pile of twisted, sleeping, naked people, and Luke instinctively turned to his partners on the floor. It was one of the women who'd made the sound caught up in a dream or, more likely, a nightmare. He turned back to find the doorframe empty, and Alastor was gone as silently and suddenly as she'd appeared. Luke reared back and threw the empty bottle across the room, where it hit the wall and exploded. Shattered glass showered down onto his partners and their whores. Samuel reacted first.

"The hell?"

He was sitting up, gun in hand as the two women resting on his chest were tossed aside, groggy and confused. The Calamity Three were never more than a reach away from their weapons, with Samuel's having been most likely stuffed in the blanket beneath his head. Paimon was slower to rise but still somehow managed to have his gun at the ready while struggling to get out from under the buxom women as they slowly roused. A freshly rolled smoke that hadn't been there a moment ago dangled from the side of his mouth.

"What is it, Luke?"

Paimon's head was on a swivel and small glass shards shook free from his hair. They sparkled like falling stars down on the two women at his feet, leaving tiny cuts across their breasts and stomach. Blood squeezed out in dark-red beads from between each micro-incision crisscrossing their pale exposed skin. The women, now fully awake, screamed as they tried to push themselves up, resulting in more cuts on their hands and knees. Glass pieces dug into their palms, embedding themselves in the meaty soft padding, and the same happened to their knees. The suddenness of it all caused the women to panic, their screams rising in intensity with each second.

They scrambled to their feet and scurried from the room without grabbing their clothes or bothering to cover themselves with their hands. The screaming continued as they rushed down the hall until the slam of a door indicated they'd retreated to one of the many other rooms. Meanwhile, the women lying with Samuel remained on the floor, cowering against each other and softly sobbing out of fright. Luke stood looking down at the two, and they clutched each other tighter.

"Well?" Luke said. "What the hell you waitin' for? Get outta' here!"

The women hurried to their feet and ran for the door, leaving their garments behind as well. Now it was Samuel and Paimon's turn to be confused as scanned the room again before turning back to Luke.

"Christ Luke," Samuel said. "What the hell's got you all worked up?"

"Boys," started Luke. "I think it's time for a change."

"Watcha' mean?" Paimon was still searching for movement in the shadows.

"We need to leave Cocytus for good."

"Leave?" Samuel wasn't expecting his fellow bandit to

say that. "Why would we do that when we have everything we need here? 'Sides, ain't no law in Cocytus to worry about."

"It's not the law that worried me." Luke paused and narrowed his eyes. "It's Lycus."

"Wait, wait?" Paimon was still awash with confusion from being jolted out of slumber. "You sayin' Lycus is some kind of lawman?"

"I swear Paimon, whatever you're smokin' is making you dumber than shit." Luke shook his head. "No, Lycus ain't no lawman, he's worse. We'd be better squaring off against a hundred sheriffs than staying here."

"Now just hold on a seco—"

"No, you *hold on,* Samuel." Luke cut him off. "I'm telling you something ain't right about this place, and I don't just mean the lack of wind. Lycus ain't tellin' us the whole truth about everything here, and he's usin' us. I don't know for what exactly, but I sure as hell don't like being on this side of things. I don't like being used."

Samuel and Paimon shared a quick glance, unsure of what their partner was getting at. Neither of them had put down or un-cocked their weapons.

"Think about it," Luke continued. "We've been out *wranglin'* these men for him, but he's never really told us why or what he's doin' with 'em. Every time we come back, he talks in circles like we're goddamned children, then pours booze down our throat and throws women at us until we're too distracted to ask any questions. Hell, none of us even really remember how we got to this place.

"And his little sidekick, or whatever the hell that girl is, she's up to something and it ain't good. She may be a witch or worse, but I ain't gonna' be schemed on by some mute freak of a little girl."

"So, what are you supposin' we do?" Samuel asked. "You want us to just pick up, leave, and never come back? That seems downright cowardly."

"No. What I'm sayin' is we leave *after* we've turned this

town upside down and taken care of Lycus along with his little bitch."

"Alright, I'm listening," Paimon said. "Whatcha' have in mind?"

"I have a plan."

# NO FUNERAL

CHERUB HADN'T INTENDED on taking Ms. Caroline up on the offer to ride back with her, but as he was gathering the food and cartridges he'd bought into a newly acquired gunny sack, she happened upon him again. He was glad for the favor this time, but didn't let on how he really felt. The path into town was a lot longer than he'd realized and would've taken him hours to walk on his own, so when she asked if he minded being protection for her on the ride again, he happily accepted.

He tried to act reluctant, and though Caroline saw right through him, she pretended not to notice. She helped tie his sack of supplies to her saddle, finding it awfully heavy. If the boy had tried to walk back home, he wouldn't have made it far having to lug the bag along with him.

"I just want to thank you again for coming along with me," Caroline said, helping him into the saddle before climbing on herself. "Can never be too careful riding along these trails. No telling who or what you might run into."

Knowing the boy was trying hard to seem mature beyond his years, she wanted to truly make him feel like she needed him for protection. The truth was Caroline always recited a well-practiced spell of protection when going to and from her home, and if someone tried to attack her, they'd very quickly realize what a mistake they'd made.

"Happy to help, ma'am," Cherub said from the saddle behind her.

"You don't have to yes and no, ma'am me. You can just call me Caroline."

"Yes Miss Caroline," he said.

She wanted to let him know he could strike the *Miss*, but decided against it upon hearing the exhaustion in the boy's voice. It was the kind of exhaustion no young boy should know, not until he's grown and on his own, but Caroline had a feeling Cherub was living a harder life than most children.

The sun was low in the sky when the two left town and the heat felt good on Cherub's back as they rode. He'd decided on the ride in he wasn't going to try to find his mother, but was starting to think he maybe should have. He passed Slim's once to get to the mercantile and again on his way back but refused to turn his head toward the building. He'd secretly hoped his mother would see him pass and come running out to hug and kiss him, but there was no such luck. Cherub would've been happy even if she ran out scolding him furiously over leaving home by himself. Anything would've been better than nothing.

A tear streaked down his dust covered cheek, which he hastily wiped away, glad to be behind Miss Caroline in the saddle so she wouldn't see. She didn't have to see to know the boy was crying, though. She could feel sadness radiating from him.

Unbeknownst to Cherub, his mother would never come running out of any place to kiss or scold him again. Emma died weeks prior by way of morphine as it finally brought her heart to a halt. She'd been dead in a room above the saloon for two days before one of the other girls discovered her in bed. Her eyes were open, her mouth agape and twisted into an expression of pain and sadness. There was nothing peaceful about the way Cherub's mother left this world.

The panicked girl screamed and ran to hold Emma, then screamed louder when she touched the cold, stiff body. Slim came running up rifle in hand thinking some drunk cowboy was beating the hell out of one of his whores, but his exasperation abated upon bursting in and seeing Emma's head cradled in the woman's arms. He wasn't surprised, and in fact expected something like this to happen much sooner, having known her addiction had grown insatiable.

Slim told one of the men at the bar he'd let him have a poke on the house if he helped take Emma's body downstairs. They carried her out back behind the saloon, where Slim unceremoniously buried her without marking the grave.

It was for the best Cherub didn't learn the truth about his mother as it would've hardened his heart beyond repair, never to be softened by love or hope again. He didn't realize how lucky it was for him to have met Miss Caroline that day, as the results of his trip to town could've ended up much different. He didn't know it, but she did. Caroline would do her best to stem the tide of what she knew lie in store for the boy, but could only prolong the inevitable for so long. She hoped, at least.

There was no stopping what was coming for Cherub.

# THE BOX

ALASTOR KNEW SHE was changing; she was getting stronger. Everything had started to come easier as far as her abilities were concerned, but she'd yet to gain full control or understanding of them. Lycus told her many times over the years of the great potential she possessed, while stressing *only he* could teach her to hone these gifts. She had no reason not to believe him, at least in the beginning, but Alastor wasn't so sure anymore.

Lycus forged a psychic bond with her as a young girl and was aware when new aspects of her power shook loose from within, but recently she'd discovered something of which he had no knowledge. The box. There was a box inside her mind Lycus could not access, and in fact did not know existed. Alastor found she was able to retreat mentally into the box to store thoughts and ideas she didn't want Lycus to know about, including the most recent enhancement of her abilities.

She could read minds with ease these days, although turning it off was harder than she'd like it to be sometimes. She didn't need to have stood in the door of the billiard room to hear what the Calamity Three were planning; she heard it blaring from Luke's mind all the way down the hall. It wasn't anything she didn't know already, and in fact Lycus told her months ago the bandits would try to double-cross him. Said he'd known it from the moment he'd met them, said it was inevitable.

## ALL OF YOUR DREAMS WILL COME TRUE

Aside from reading thoughts, Alastor discovered she had the ability to probe minds. She could poke around from the inside, pull the chords, cross the wires, potentially cause a meltdown. She hadn't tried to go that deep yet despite the compulsion, because she kept this talent locked away in the box. Lycus knew she was an adept telepath, but not that she could cause physical damage to someone's brain by way of her thoughts alone. Alastor planned to keep it that way until she felt more confident of her control over it. One thing Lycus taught her was to *never* trust anybody, and while it went unsaid, the implication was it applied to him as well. Alastor took that to heart.

She believed there could come a day when the two would be adversaries. She tried to suppress the idea any time it snuck into her mind, but was unable to dismiss the notion entirely. Alastor couldn't imagine a scenario in which she and Lycus would become enemies. Or maybe she didn't want to. What could cause such a rift in their relationship as to pit them against one another? She was careful to leave her feelings regarding the subject in the box, not wanting her insecurities around the matter broadcast directly into her mentor's mind.

She went downstairs on her way to Lycus's master bedroom, which took up the majority of the lower east wing. She'd been careful to seal away her secret thoughts in the box before approaching the partially open door, and as she went to knock Lycus called out before her she could announce her presence.

"Come in, Alastor."

She pushed the door open and stepped into the dark, over-sized, mammoth of a room. This was one of the illusions of the house as this area appeared much smaller from the outside. Inside, the ceiling was higher than the second story roof, and the sprawling depth of the chamber went on until disappearing in the darkness. Lycus sat in another of his favorite high-back chairs facing an even bigger fireplace than what was in the living room.

"Alastor," he said without turning around. "Where were you just now?"

She paused, her approach confused by the question. He knew she'd gone upstairs to check in on the bandits, and even if he didn't know beforehand, he'd see it in her mind. She didn't understand what exactly he was driving at.

"Not when you were upstairs," he continued. "Before you came to the door, you were somewhere else. Somewhere I couldn't see you."

Alastor kept her body language from betraying the surge of panic triggered by Lycus's question hoping he didn't see it in her eyes as she stepped around the chair to face him. Was it possible she'd been wrong about the box? What if he'd been able to access it all along and already knew what she'd been keeping from him?

"What are you hiding from me, Alastor? More importantly though, why? I didn't think we kept secrets from each other, but lately it seems maybe I was wrong."

Lycus's coal-black eyes narrowed as he leveled them on Alastor. He was attempting to rip the truth from her head, only he couldn't. She felt him probing her mind, searching for an answer impossible to find. He might suspect something but knew nothing for sure, and she tried to steer him back on course by focusing on what Luke was planning.

"I already know what those three aim to do, goddamnit." Lycus stood towering over the girl and pointed his club-like finger in her face. "Hell, I already told you it was gonna' happen! Now, you better tell me what you're keepin' from me, girl, 'fore I really start to get angry."

She felt him aggressively attempt to force himself deeper into her mind, to no avail. She *knew* he couldn't get to the box and rising confidence replaced her quickly evaporating fear. She'd become overtaken by the exhilaration of the feeling and didn't realize what she'd done until she saw the look in his eyes. It had been a reflex, a new and unexpected reaction. She'd quickly pulled back, but not quick enough. Alastor had pushed Lycus back with her mind and he felt it.

The two stared at each other, stunned for different reasons, waiting to see who would make the next move. Lycus opened his mouth just as a loud crash followed by gunfire drew their attention to the door. Lycus and Alastor shared another short glance before unholstering their guns and heading for the commotion, but the confrontation was far from over.

# TRICK SHOT

THE INITIAL JOVIALNESS Magoth projected at the start had all but dried up since Lloyd advanced in the game. The cocksure attitude and warped smile were replaced with brooding and a scowl, and his stubby arms remained crossed against his chest as he stared a hole of hate through Lloyd whose upbeat attitude served to further needle the tiny game master. Even so, he remained cautious and kept an eye out for the other shoe to drop.

Lloyd could shoot, and whoever set him up in this game knew as much, but it couldn't be this easy. There had to be more to it, otherwise what was the point? Even now, the purpose of being in Cocytus to play a game was nebulous at best, but someone knew exactly what they were doing, and it was being done for a specific purpose. Lloyd didn't know what that was either but had a feeling he wouldn't understand. Bottom line was somebody needed *him* for something important, and he'd be damned if he let them have him without a fight. Whatever the plan, Lloyd aimed to dismantle it, after he'd found his gun, of course.

"Slowing down Lloyd?" Magoth hissed. "You've been taking your sweet time with this one. What's the matter? The great gunfighter finally stumped?"

Lloyd wasn't stumped, he was stalling to give himself more time to think on the riddle of his being there. He'd taken several long looks into the distance around the range searching for anything out of the ordinary to catch his attention that could work to his advantage.

"I don't know, Maggot." Lloyd smiled. "You might have me on this one."

"Magoth*!*"

Lloyd smiled again. So far, each part of the game involved trick-shooting, which Lloyd thought was fine and all, but still a far cry from the talent of a gunfighter such as himself. He'd picked up quite a bit of practice doing some trick-shooting when passing through certain towns over the years while out on jobs. There were some places, especially in Texas, where they took trick-shooting mighty serious and winning competitions were coveted points of pride amongst cowboys of the region.

Lloyd was a great shot. It wasn't hard for him to pick up the tricks of the trade when it came to competitive shooting, but he never aimed to be the best. He would enter the trick-shot contests for the prize money, which he would then promptly steal by way of a holdup upon being eliminated. It happened like that more times than not, but after a while Lloyd started to outright win legitimately, which turned out to be fun for him. He started actually trying to win rather than waiting to blow it so he could steal the pot, and now he was glad he did.

The shot he was about to take consisted of using a Winchester rifle to shoot a tin can off a wooden post five feet away. The catch was the target was behind Lloyd, and he was permitted to shoot forward only. Hitting something by shooting in the opposite direction of your target sounds like an impossible exercise in futility but is really one of the older trick-shots out there. It's not well known since those who've perfected it keep their methods close to the vest so as not to give an edge to their competitors.

Lloyd learned it when squaring off against one of these so-called gatekeepers of trick-shooting who thought they were a master at hiding what they did. They weren't. Lloyd picked up on every subtle flick of the wrist, slide of the finger, and movement of his hands, having deconstructed the man's methods on the first try. It was like a magic trick in that once you know how it's done, you can't believe you ever fell for it. This particular shot was far easier than it looked, which only made it that much harder.

Lloyd paced the length of the wooden rail that marked where he was to stand, looking out past the game into the darkness of the desert. A pang wrenched his heart when he realized he had no idea if he was in Texas anymore.

"No more stalling, Lloyd." Magoth was smiling again now, though not as wide as, but he was regaining confidence with each moment Lloyd didn't take the shot. "You have nothing to be ashamed of, really. I certainly didn't think you'd make it this far; in fact, *nobody* makes it this far. Ever. So, why not just take your bes—"

Lloyd rested the rifle over his shoulder and turned to face Magoth so the barrel pointed out at the range behind him, then pulled the trigger. The bullet whizzed out into the distance, but it didn't matter where it ended up. The important thing was the open-hipped stance he'd taken, the angle at which the rifle was placed over his shoulder, and the precise spot he'd stopped along the rail before taking the shot. This was the exact place *and* position he needed to be standing in for the casing to eject at the right trajectory to strike the lip of the can and knock it off the post.

This time Lloyd didn't smile or even grin despite having advanced in the game once again. His face hardened into stern features, incapable of expressing the fear he no longer felt. What he was being put through was called a 'game', but he wanted it known he was taking it more seriously than anything in his life prior. Magoth's smile retreated, seemingly for good, and his eyes burned with molten, frenzied anger. Lloyd dropped the rifle in the dirt at the dwarf's feet.

"I don't know who you *think* you are, Mr. Gunfighter, but this does not end well for you." Magoth's voice was pitched deeper and sounded like a tiger had been clawing at his vocal cords. "I've seen what happens. I've always seen it, and it's always the same. So go ahead Lloyd, win. Keep winning and get to the end because the results never change."

Lloyd was glad he'd dropped the rifle, otherwise he'd have buried the butt between Magoth's eyes, but he stayed calm and focused. The small man wouldn't be saying any of this to him if he weren't rattled and scared. He wasn't supposed to get as far as he had, which was already farther than anyone else by Magoth's own admission. Whatever lie at the end was *not* certain. Lloyd was rewriting the conclusion of the story with each shot.

"If you know so much, then why're you gettin' worked up?" Lloyd finally allowed himself to smile as he broke eye contact to look back down the range. "Seems like there's no point to bein' upset if you already know I can't win. What's the harm in playin' along and lettin' me have a little fun on the way to my demise?"

"You *will* lose, gunfighter." Magoth practically growled, as if reverting to a feral state. "It's not a matter of what I know or don't know. It already is."

"Since you're so confident, I guess you won't mind us movin' along to the next shot, then."

Lloyd walked toward the start of his next challenge and didn't look back when he heard the dwarf running up on him from behind.

# SUPPERTIME

CHERUB AND MISS CAROLINE sparked up a close friendship, though she nearly had to trick him into it. She'd dropped him at his house after the first trip they'd taken to town together, but ended up coming back a few hours later. Caroline didn't ask the boy if she *could* come back knowing he'd put up a fight, so she just did it and was glad she had upon entering the house. She knew the way to the boy's heart would be through his stomach and made a meal of cornbread and vegetable stew to smooth over her impromptu visit.

Cherub heard her horse and stood in the open doorway, watching her approach from the concealing darkness. Caroline didn't realize he was there until she'd dismounted and was almost to the door and even then, only because he spoke out.

"What're you doin' here?"

Caroline jumped from the start but composed herself quickly, holding the basket of food up in front of her.

"I wanted to show my appreciation for you keeping an eye out for me on our way to town and back," she said. "I made some stew with vegetables from my garden, and there's some freshly baked cornbread in there as well."

Cherub stared at the basket rather than taking it. She could see the hungry look on the boy's face, only he didn't know how to react to the gesture of kindness. He was conflicted between being the tough and strong man of the house he wanted to be who didn't need help or charity, and the hungry, scared child he was. Caroline smiled as she brushed past him into the dark dwelling without giving him a chance to stop her.

The small house was dark and cold despite the warmth of the season, and the overwhelming lingering sadness that permeated everything was nearly too much for the empath witch to take. Caroline managed to stay herself and removed the candles from the basket, now glad she'd decided to include them, having had a feeling they'd come in handy. She lit the first one and the light it cast seemed to only make the house feel darker and smaller.

She placed it at the center of the table before lighting a second and then a third, positioning them in places where they'd provide the most light. Cherub stood by the table; his eyes fixed upon the basket which she'd set down. He hadn't seen the inside of the house at night in weeks and forgot how much difference a few flickering flames made, but it barely registered with his hunger having usurped the entirety of his attention. Cherub had bought some food stuffs earlier that day in town, but it was only a couple loaves of bread and a block of cheese. He couldn't remember the last time he'd had an actual prepared meal.

Caroline pulled out one of the chairs for Cherub to sit while she unpacked the food. She'd wrapped the boiling hot stew well, so it retained its warmth, which was a good thing since there was no fireplace inside the home over which it could be heated. She unwrapped the cornbread and Cherub ripped a piece off, shoving it whole into his mouth before she could set the loaf on the table.

"Sorry," Cherub said, looking down ashamed of the impulse like he'd done something wrong.

"Sorry for what?" Caroline laughed. "No reason to apologize for being a hungry growing boy, I mean, young man."

Cherub didn't notice being called a kid or, if so, didn't care anymore. His eyes were glued to the pot of stew as Caroline set it down in front of him. When she removed the lid, steam licked out over the side and rose like apparitions escaping the boiling pits of hell. The delicious aroma of the witch's blended herbs and vegetable mixture overpowered the staleness in the house and pushed the old air out to make room for the delectable smell of hot food. She placed a wooden spoon next to the pot while Cherub continued to stare, his mouth visibly watering.

"You can go ahead," Caroline said. "I've already eaten. I brought this all for you."

Cherub didn't waste any more time with objections or questions and instead snatched the spoon and commenced shoveling the food into his mouth. It was hot and burned his tongue, but he couldn't stop himself. At that moment, it was the best food he'd ever eaten in his short life so far and he reveled in each flavor-packed spoonful. Caroline lit another candle while the boy ate and looked at what else the tiny domicile consisted of.

"This may be a silly question, you being so independent and all," she said, entering the short hallway, "but do you live here alone? I mean, do your parents live here as well?"

"No."

The monosyllabic response was the only answer he gave between spoonfuls of stew, and Caroline wasn't sure what part of the question he was answering. She decided to wait until he finished, or at least slowed down to ask again, though she knew the answers just by looking around. She approached one of the two closed doors and slowly pushed it open, holding the candle up, seeing the room was ransacked.

Broken jagged pieces of what was once a wooden chair were strewn across a floor covered in wadded filthy dresses, slips, ripped up bustles, and other unidentifiable articles of clothing. The bedding was twisted and tangled in a heap where it radiated a foul mixed aroma of chemical-sweat and sex. She recognized it immediately. The pieces were falling into place now for Caroline and finding no sign of a man present in the house explained Cherub's attempt at advanced maturation.

She looked in the other room, the one where Cherub slept on the floor, and her heart broke a little more for him. His bed consisted of a small patch of straw covered by a single sheet with an equally thin blanket tossed off to the side. Next to the makeshift bed were several boxes of cartridges for Cherub's Colt stacked neatly against the wall. The gun belt he'd had double-cinched around his waist earlier hung from a nail in the wall above the boxes. Aside from those few items, there was nothing else in the boy's room.

Caroline pulled the door closed and went back out to the kitchen where Cherub was jamming the last hunk of cornbread into his mouth. She saw the pot of stew was empty as well, reaffirming her decision to bring food to the boy was a good one. She'd brought enough for what she thought would last at least three meals, but he clearly hadn't been eating well or regularly for a while. There was plenty more where that came from, though, and she'd be happy to bring it to him. Cherub looked up as she approached, and again his expression changed to reflect shame and embarrassment over having made a glutton of himself, but Caroline smiled as if it was perfectly normal for a boy to eat an entire meal for three in one sitting.

"How did you like it?" She asked, taking the seat across from him at the table.

"Good, thank you ma'am I mean, Miss Caroline." Cherub wiped the back of his hand across his mouth.

"Is that your mother's room back there?" Caroline went back to her questions hoping a full stomach would make the boy less reticent about answering, but she could already see the far-off look in Cherub's eyes as he processed the question.

"Yes."

"Does your father live here as well?"

"No." Cherub shook his head. "My pa left a long time ago."

"You never knew him then?"

"No, but I know he was a great gunfighter and I aim to be just as good or better."

The picture of Cherub's life was becoming clearer and his wearing a gun around that was almost as long as his torso made perfect sense. His father was long gone, and his mother wasn't around much or had abandoned him altogether. Either way, Caroline didn't need to ask if Cherub's mother used morphine with the stench of addiction wafting from her room.

"Where's your mother now, then? Does she work in town, or is she . . . "

Caroline trailed off, realizing her phrasing carried an implication of prostitution she hadn't intended. She was just trying to get information out of the boy without riling him into being defensive. Either the meal had worked as the intoxicating truth serum she'd hoped it would be, or he'd simply resigned to telling her what she wanted to know, but either way he didn't hold back.

"I don't know really," he started. "I haven't seen her in a while, but far as I know she works for Slim selling pokes."

Caroline was taken aback by the nonchalance with which he spoke of his mother's profession. No ten-year-old boy should know what a 'poke' is, let alone be aware his own mother was 'selling' them. She wanted to believe he really didn't know and was repeating things he'd heard in order to sound more grown up, but in her heart, she knew he knew. Having knowledge of these things so young would leave a permanent dark blotch on his soul for as long as he lived, which she unfortunately knew how *long* that would be.

"When was the last time she's been here to the house?" Caroline asked, trying to steer the conversation away from talk of his mother's whoring. "Looks to me like you've been on your own here for quite a while, not that you can't handle it, of course."

Cherub acted like he was thinking, even though he knew the answer.

"Goin' on three weeks now, I suppose."

Caroline was again left aghast at the boy's response and tried hard not to let it show, though the anger she felt towards a woman she'd never met was steadily building. Cherub was obviously emaciated, and she wondered how many of those days over the last three weeks he'd gone without eating at all, but glad not to know. The answer would only add fuel to the fire of fury she felt at the mistreatment of the boy.

"That's a long time for anyone to be on their own," she said. "I don't care who you are."

Cherub answered with a shrug, followed by a silence Caroline struggled to fill until struck with a realization. The best way to protect the boy would be to keep him close to her, and she knew just how to do it.

"I'd like to hire you, Cherub," she finally said.

"Hire me? Hire me for what . . . protection?"

His tone indicated not even he believed she wanted to pay a child to protect her.

"No," she started. "I mean, yes, that as well, but I've got a lot of vegetables to harvest from my garden. It's not very big but keeps me a lot busier than I'd like to be, and with you being so close, I figured I'd offer you the job before I went lookin' for anyone else."

Cherub's lips parted, but no sound came from his mouth as he tried to make sense of what was being asked of him.

"We could figure out the best way to compensate you, and of course you'd have all the vegetables you can eat."

He perked up at the mention of a steady food supply as Caroline continued.

"And I could even partially pay you with rounds for that Colt of yours if you'd like. I'm sure a gunfighter in training such as yourself can never have too many bullets. Am I right?"

The change in his expression and body language undeniably communicated his interest. He practically had to clap his hand over his mouth to keep the word 'yes' from jumping out before she finished her sentence. She had to give him credit, though. For a young boy, he was able to compose himself before answering with a far better poker face than the most degenerate of gamblers could hope to perfect in their lifetime.

"Well, I do have my responsibilities 'round here," Cherub started. "But I reckon I'll take you up on your offer. Why, it'd be almost downright rude of me not to, wouldn't it?"

"I wouldn't want you to . . . " Caroline paused to gesture around the hardly habitable hovel, "shirk your duty to your own homestead. I wouldn't want you to take the job because you feel *obligated* to help because I'm a woman alone. I can handle it on my own just fine until I find someone. That is, unless you're sure you ca—"

"I'm sure! I'll do it!"

Cherub cut her off, unable to hold back this time, and Caroline smiled at his excitement. He was just a boy, after all, and it finally showed through the external veneer of adulthood he'd put upon himself.

"I mean, I'm sure it won't be a problem at all. I'd be happy to do it. I want to."

Caroline stood and nodded.

"Good then," she said. "You'd better get some sleep because we'll need to start at first light tomorrow."

"Yes, ma'—Miss Caroline," Cherub said standing as well.

Caroline put the empty stew pot in the basket and headed for the front door, pausing to turn back before leaving.

"You know the way, yes?"

Cherub nodded.

"It's only a few miles and you'll be able to see the garden from the path. The walk isn't bad and will do well to limber you up before the work begins."

"I'll be there." Cherub nodded again. "Thank you, Miss Caroline."

Caroline smiled and turned to leave, but it fell from her face the moment she stepped outside. She saw Cherub's unavoidable fate flash across her mind again, stripping away the small bit of hope she'd foolishly built up. Rather than leaving her sad this time, she was angry. It'd been building since she'd learned of Cherub's mother's negligence, and now a full-blown rage bubbled over from within the witch.

# AND THEN THERE WERE TWO

**LYCUS PUSHED PAST** Alastor, gun in hand, and sprinted up the stairs. He wasn't happy about being interrupted in the middle of their discussion, as it would have to wait for the time being, but would not be forgotten. He was fully prepared to confront her with the topic again as soon as he'd remedied the distraction. Lycus knew Alastor was getting stronger and would continue to do so, and while that meant she could potentially be more powerful than himself, he didn't think it would be something he'd have to contend with so soon.

He hadn't counted on her keeping things from him having the ability to block him out completely. More worrisome was the pushback he'd felt from Alastor. It was only for a moment, but still a powerful taste of her capabitlies. She'd been holding back. He hadn't predicted she'd be able to wield her thoughts to the extent of causing physical damage so early on in her development, and he cursed himself for not paying closer attention.

He hadn't been lazy, but distracted having to split his focus across the several irons he had in the fire with being so close to the end goal. He'd labored for years to get back to Oblivion, and now he could almost taste it, as Behemoth was already being drawn to the hole between worlds that was Cocytus. Soon the massive creature would barrel through the opening, pulling all of hell with it.

If it took Lycus this long to discover Alastor was keeping something from him, what was to say he hadn't missed anything else along the way? He was forced to consider the possibility someone or something was potentially trying to ruin his work by throwing everything out of alignment, and that someone could very well be Alastor.

He would not abide this type of misfortune to befall him and was prepared to kill everyone in Cocytus, his young mock-protégé included. Nothing would stop him from getting back home.

He made the turn at the landing with Alastor a step behind him, and the two were shoulder to shoulder as they reached the hall and sprinted toward the billiard room. A door on the right opened just enough for the women hiding inside to see them run by. The two women, still without their clothes, rushed from the room to escape by way of the stairs. A second door opened and slammed behind them as the other two women followed suit, running naked to the stairs.

Lycus lengthened his gate overtaking Alastor by a step and plunged through the open doorway first, his pistol at the ready.

"What in the hell is goin' on up here? Who the hell started the goddamn shootin'?"

What he found inside was a confusing sight. Broken glass and splintered pieces of wood from a busted table were strewn across the room while Samuel and Paimon stood naked limply clutching guns in hands attached to arms that hung slack at their side. The two were in shock, mouths agape as they stared at the floor in front of them. Lycus followed their gaze down to the take in the scene.

Luke was lying face down and motionless amidst the scattered debris. A crimson bloom in the center of his back pushed enough blood out to form a small puddle around his torso, but the flow had ceased indicating the man's heart had stopped. Lycus fought to keep from bursting into laughter as he looked back up at what was left of the Calamity Three.

“Shit boys,” Said Lycus. “Now, why in the hell did you do that?”

Neither of the men said anything and kept staring down at Luke’s body like they expected him to jump up and answer the question. Alastor stood behind Lycus with a pistol in each hand trained on the men while probing their minds for exactly what had happened.

“We . . . ” Samuel started. “We didn’t do nothin’.”

“It . . . it was . . . ” Paimon choked. “He ain’t dead, really, is he?”

They were actually telling the truth, which Alastor found odd, since it was probably the first time in their lives they’d done so. She allowed Lycus to see what she’d seen in their minds, hoping it would show she wasn’t holding anything back, but also because it didn’t appear as if the remaining bandits would be able to articulate the details anytime soon.

“He shot his goddamn self!” Samuel shouted. “His own goddamn self!”

Samuel wasn’t wrong. Luke had been responsible for his own death, only it wasn’t done on purpose. It seemed the amount of drinking he’d done had gotten on top of him all at once, what with the strength of Lycus’s special custom spirits. His whiskey was far stronger than any you’d find outside Cocytus, and it was possible his tolerance was lowered having been away for a month drinking common man’s bourbon.

What happened was no dignified death for an outlaw such as Luke, but perhaps the most poetically just. He’d been riled and angry since they’d arrived back in Cocytus and handled it by drinking nearly non-stop since walking into the house. Instead of eating, Luke drank, instead of fucking Luke drank, and instead of sleeping, Luke drank. It was only a matter of time before even a man the likes of him would succumb to the powerful tonic’s effect.

# ALL OF YOUR DREAMS WILL COME TRUE

It happened shortly after Luke stood up, broke the bottle, and began laying out his plan to leave Cocytus. He was in mid-sentence when his head began to swim, and darkness rushed in, quickly blotting out consciousness. He was out cold but alive until he hit the floor. Luke kept the hammer pulled back on his pistol nearly always as most outlaws and bandits did to save a fraction of a second when drawing on someone. It proved the difference between life and death more often than not.

Luke must've loosened his gun belt, or got it twisted up while he was sitting somehow, or maybe as he fell through the table in front of him the gun was re-situated on impact. Whatever the case, the barrel ended up pointing up into his sternum and discharged when he landed on top of it. The single bullet pierced Luke's heart exploding the vital organ killing him instantly.

When Lycus saw what Alastor showed him, he could no longer hold back his laughter. It was an unexpected but welcome turn of events that reaffirmed his confidence. The Calamity Three posed a potential threat to his plan if they turned on him like they wanted to, and now one of them was dead on the floor having accidentally shot himself *while* planning said betrayal. It didn't get any better than having the Universe unknowingly take care of your dirty work for you.

Lycus approached the body and bent down, pretending to check for a pulse before standing back up to deliver a hard kick to the corpse's ribs. The impact caused a gout of blood to spray up from the bullet hole like a whale emptying its spout.

"Well boys," Lycus said to Samuel and Paimon. "Looks like you two are gonna need to change your name."

# THE STARS AT NIGHT ARE BIG AND BRIGHT

MAGOTH SPRINTED UP behind Lloyd as he approached the next challenge, not to launch an attack from behind, but to cut him off from the game.

"Oh, Lloyd," Magoth sang, his voice having resumed its soft jovial lilt. "I'm afraid this one requires a bit more explanation than those prior."

The small man was surprisingly fast, and Lloyd nearly walked into him as Magoth jumped out in front. He scowled down at him then looked out at the range. He didn't see any new targets and had a feeling it meant things weren't going to be so easy from here on out.

"So," Lloyd spat. "Explain."

"This challenge is on the cerebral side of things." Magoth talked through his widening smile. "That means you'll have to use your noodle!"

The dwarf pulled himself up and sat on the wood railing in front of Lloyd and gave a sweeping performative gesture to the range before them.

"What do you see, Lloyd?"

Lloyd already knew what he saw but scanned the area again for something he might've missed.

"I don't see a goddamn thing. What am I supposed to do? Imagine a target to shoot? And where's the gun?"

He stepped back and looked around for a weapon but found none. Magoth reached behind his back and his hand returned holding a pistol he'd seemingly pulled from thin air. The gun was one Lloyd had seen before but never fired. It was an Ordinance Revolver made by the Swiss to specifically be lighter for military use. It even required a specific cartridge made just for the pistol.

Lloyd shot a man in a holdup a year ago for mouthing off, and when he went to rifle through his coat, found an Ordinance concealed in a side holster. The gun was lighter than any pistol he'd held before, and it felt wrong in his hand. It was *too* light. It felt like a child's toy that would break to pieces when he pulled the trigger. He left it behind but did take a small sack of gold pieces from the man's coat pocket, so it wasn't all bad.

He took the gun from Magoth and it felt lighter than he remembered. A quick check of the cylinder confirmed it was loaded with only one bullet. Lloyd passed the gun back and forth from one hand to the other and attempted to reposition his grip on the handle a few different ways but couldn't get comfortable holding the thing. He'd fired a lot of guns, but not this one, and its many variables put him at a severe disadvantage.

He had no knowledge of the weapon's range, didn't know if the aim was true, or what the kick was like if there even was one. Lloyd again contemplated pressing the Ordinance against Magoth's nose using the single bullet to rid himself of the annoying game master but stayed the urge. He knew he'd shaken Magoth's confidence. He *knew* he was doing something right. Otherwise, why would he lose his temper over Lloyd winning if he was going to be killed no matter how he fared in the ridiculous game? He couldn't give up now. He had to keep playing. Lloyd continued examining the gun trying to act like nothing was wrong.

"So, what's the game?" He finally said.

"Look."

Magoth pointed to the sky, and Lloyd looked up. He saw nothing at first, but then five stars in a line started burning brighter than any others. They'd taken on different hues as well, changing from white to red, blue, green, orange, and purple, respectively. All five stars, now distinct from one another by color, started to fall.

"Listen closely and carefully, because I'm not going to repeat myself," Magoth started, his sinister tone having returned. "Five stars are falling, falling in the night. Only one's important though, so hope that you choose right. First, fix your view on the second to the left, before it changes places in line with all the rest. When it locks in place, count three stars to the right. That's the one to follow now, so keep it in your sights. When it switches places, count two back to the left, but keep your eye on this one now, it's not yet time to rest. And as they plunge to earth before impact is made, count three to the right and pull the trigger. A direct hit will make you a winner."

"Wait, count what now?"

Magoth smiled, shook his head, and pointed back to the falling stars. Lloyd snapped his head up just in time to see them start to move from their initial formation. He pointed the ultra-light pistol up at the sky using the barrel keep track of what he hoped was the correct star. They moved faster the further they fell, and Lloyd rattled off out loud under his breath what he hoped was the correct order of Magoth's sing-song instructions, but his gut told him he was off. He'd skipped something or miscounted. Either way, he'd missed a step somewhere, and there was no time to go through the rhyme again.

The stars were too close to the ground to backtrack and correct his mistake. Lloyd had to shoot one and shoot it right goddamn now. He pointed the barrel at the star he'd settled on, the red one, but switched at the last moment to the blue star on its right. Lloyd gently squeezed the trigger of the Swiss-made revolver, hoping he'd chosen right.

# I HEAR YOU KNOCKIN'

**BERTIE JUMPED WHEN** the pounding started. Someone on the other side very badly wanted to come back through, but he was absolutely *not* opening the door. There've been people in the past who'd tried to come back, not often, but it did happen. These attempts happened within moments of the door closing, and even then, the person got only three or four good bangs on the thing before being pulled into their game.

No one had been through the door in hours though, and this desperate pounding started suddenly growing more feverishly urgent by the second. It was maddening and induced a spike in the Englishman's anxiety. Lycus told Bertie not to let Lloyd back through the door, but what if it wasn't Lloyd? He'd been in there quite a while already, and it didn't make sense for it to be him, but it didn't make sense for it to be anyone.

The knocking turned frantic, and the door shook violently on its hinges from the increasing fervor with which it came. Bertie couldn't take it anymore. He looked down the hallway and considered sprinting to the other door but thought better of it knowing he'd be blamed and punished if someone came back through, and he wasn't there to stop them, or at least report it to Lycus so he could take care of it.

He turned back and approached the door slowly, his hand out in front of him, trembling uncontrollably. Bertie didn't realize he'd made the decision to open it until his fingers were nearly touching the knob. The closer he got, the harder he shook and had to grip his forearm with his other hand to hold it steady. The pounding continued louder and harder, and the doorknob vibrated so intensely he could hardly close his hand around it to turn.

When he did, the door burst open, and Bertie knew he'd made a mistake. Standing on the other side was Lloyd with a gun leveled at his head.

# WHAT'S BEHIND DOOR NUMBER ONE?

LLOYD FIRED AND the blue star flattened and stretched to the size and shape of a door, which immediately flew open to reveal the Englishman he'd met in the gambling hall standing on the other side. Bertie was the man's name. The look on his face was like that of a child getting caught with his hand in the cookie jar. Despite his lack of experience with the Swiss revolver, Lloyd's aim was true. A small red hole appeared between Bertie's eyes and blood spilled from the wound like an open faucet covering his face in a crimson film.

Bertie rocked on his feet for a moment before falling forward face first to the desert floor. The sand soaked up the blood greedily in the space between granules before it had a chance to pool around the Englishman's head. The door slammed shut and disintegrated into dust on the wind, along with the other four fallen stars. Lloyd stared at the dead man lying ten feet in front of him, confused at what had taken place. He examined the gun and smelled the barrel to make sure it *actually* fired. Turned out he'd been right about the pistol's recoil being nearly non-existent. Magoth, still perched on the railing, somehow managed to keep his balance as he rocked with laughter.

He doubled over, stubby fat fingers clutching his paunchy stomach, and continued to howl, having found the outcome of the game especially funny. Lloyd couldn't tell if the reaction was a result of him having picked wrong, or if Magoth found the Englishman's death funny. There was always a chance it was both. Lloyd dropped the Ordinance and stepped back to put some space between him and Magoth in case he had to run. If he really was supposed to die, he for damn sure wasn't just going to roll over and make it easy on them.

"Well?" Lloyd finally said.

Magoth's laughter started to taper off as if he were about to answer but instead burst into another giggle fit. Lloyd was prepared for the worst and ready to hightail it out into the dark desert on foot. He'd rather die out in the wilderness alone than be strangled by a man less than half his size. Lloyd edged back another step, waiting for the laughter to subside before jumping to any conclusions.

"Well?" Lloyd repeated. "I'm talkin' to you, you giggly bastard. Did I shoot the right one, or what?"

Magoth narrowed his eyes while slowly shaking his head. His smile, having departed with the laughter, twisted back into an aggressive snarl.

"What do you think, gunfighter?"

# RETURN TO SENDER

BERTIE WAS DEAD before realizing he'd been shot. The Swiss revolver was smaller and lighter, but still a military weapon designed to do real damage. The specially made bullet penetrated the thickest part of his skull with ease and broke into several pieces as it entered his brain.

The fragments ricocheted around inside his skull, burning off their kinetic energy while scrambling his brain to the extent it was unable to sustain life. The Englishman felt nothing as his lifeless body pitched forward through the open door and into the dessert.

While Bertie was lucky enough to pass painlessly into death, what waited for him on the other side would be nothing but. Lycus had plucked him from endless punishment and the Abomination charged with doling it out. Bertie had been gone long enough to almost forget what an eternity of suffering was like, but it all came rushing back upon his return to death.

Bertie opened his mouth to curse Lycus, curse Cocytus, and curse the man who shot him, but instead of sound came the hundred thousand fire ants already eating him from the inside out.

# A LONG AND THOUGHTFUL EVENING

LYCUS SAT BEHIND the large desk in his personal study, which was accessible only from within the wing of the house serving as his living quarters. He'd had the desk made special for him up north and the Calamity Three were charged with picking it up and bringing it back while out on a wrangle. It had to be made from oak, *had* to, and there was nothing but pine in Texas and death in Cocytus, so Lycus had the desk commissioned. He remembered Luke bitched the most and loudest about having to haul the desk on a cart all the way through the desert. Lycus smiled at the thought of not having to hear Luke complain about anything anymore.

He spun in his chair to look out the window behind him and watched Samuel and Paimon atop their horses, dragging Luke's body with them. The corpse was tied by his feet, and while most of the body was covered by a burlap sack, there wasn't one big enough to fit the entirety of the hulking frame, so Luke's legs were completely exposed. The men moved slowly toward the outskirts of town to bury their fallen partner where Lycus guessed Samuel and Paimon would most likely discuss at length what their next move was going to be, a move undoubtedly to be made against him. Whatever they decided was of no consequence now.

Without Luke, the Calamity Three were hobbled like a

hydra missing a head, and this time it wasn't going to grow back. The two men alone were useless. They knew their parts in the scheme of things, but not much else. Neither had the understanding or wherewithal to put it all together, and Lycus couldn't imagine the men attempting a coup as a duo. They needed a decisive voice of direction to organize their actions and they didn't have one anymore. Without it, they were likely to shoot their own peckers off trying to do a job with just the two of them.

When the men were far enough away to have disappeared into the dark Cocytus night, Lycus turned around in his chair and reached for a box of cigars on his desk. He selected one, bit the tip off, spitting it on the floor, and struck a match against the arm of his chair. He touched the flame the cigar and puffed it to life from the opposite end while slowly rotating the thing between his fingers. When it was evenly lit, Lycus tossed the spent matchstick into an ornate glass ashtray next to the cigar box, leaned back in his chair, and became lost in thought as he smoked.

Alastor had helped carry Luke's body outside and assisted in tying it to the men's saddles, but rather than continuing their discussion from earlier in the evening Lycus sent the girl to bed. He didn't have to tell her the conversation would resume in the morning. She knew the subject would need to be addressed and resolved to Lycus's satisfaction, from that there was no getting out of. While Alastor was indeed in bed in the room directly across from Lycus's quarters, she was far from sleep, and he could sense her restless apprehension.

In the morning, he would approach the issue from an entirely different angle. He let his anger get the better of him earlier, which put Alastor immediately on the defensive. Despite having done her best to shield her thoughts, she didn't pull back fast enough, and he felt her fear from his accusation. Was she afraid because she'd been caught, and if so, what did she think she'd been caught doing? More alarming to Lycus was the actual physical force she'd been able to generate with her mind, which had the potential of becoming a major problem if not addressed.

Alastor wouldn't be afraid unless she *knew* what she was doing was wrong. The girl had never lied to him in all the years he'd been raising her, and why she would feel the need to suddenly start worried him. Maybe he'd misinterpreted the visions he'd seen warning him of the trouble coming to Cocytus? He initially saw the Calamity Three eventually becoming a thorn in his side, but perhaps he'd been wrong? Could it be Alastor who would turn on him in the eleventh hour and undo all the hard work he'd done? Work she herself played a significant part in?

It was difficult for Lycus to accept this as a possibility, and twenty-four hours ago he wouldn't have even entertained the thought but being forced to consider it was tantamount to heartbreak. If the largest threat to Lycus's plan was currently in bed across the hall, it meant he himself had sealed his own downfall upon his subsequent acquisition of the girl. It wasn't wandering the desert alone that he'd happened upon Alastor. That was only a fabricated memory he'd planted in the girl after kidnapping her from a coven he'd happened upon one night. His initial plan was to use the girl as a bargaining chip to extort the witches for their help with settling Cocytus, but his plan changed when he realized what he had in Alastor.

Lycus briefly considered the trouble coming from someone on the other side, the very home he longed to return to, and he was being sabotaged by one of his detractors and their cohorts. He'd been careful every step of the way certain he'd taken all necessary steps to conceal his actions keeping himself and Cocytus cloaked against his enemies until it was too late. He called out to Behemoth and Behemoth only but was it possible another Abomination had intercepted his signal and used the link to Cocytus to not only thwart Lycus's plan, but destroy him entirely in the process.

The worst part of all was Alastor could be in on it. An abomination in disguise playing the long con over years so Lycus would never see it coming. If that was true, he now had the time and opportunity to defend himself.

There was a chance, albeit slight, none of what he suspected of Alastor was true. He wanted to think she was just confused about her ever strengthening abilities, unsure how to communicate her feelings to him. The girl couldn't talk after all, but it never stopped her from sharing with Lycus in the past, and she'd never been afraid to ask him questions about anything. Hell, he was practically her father, although he'd made it very clear he wasn't and did not want her to start thinking of him as a parental figure. He more likened their relationship to that of business partners or at least something along the lines of an employer and employee. Lycus was able to make that distinction and keep the relationship compartmentalized, but he couldn't speak for the girl. She was either with him or against him, and he aimed to find out for sure once the sun rolled out the new day.

In the room across the hall Alastor was restless, unable to sleep, and she'd retreated into her box to think privately about the impending confrontation the morning would bring. For the first time in their relationship Alastor considered the possibility of Lycus *not* having her best interests in mind, and rather than feeling fear over the thought she felt anger, only wasn't quite sure why.

Lycus had always been up front with her about his plan for bringing his homeland Hellscape into the world he'd been banished to and loathed being stuck there. She was being used by him to bolster and strengthen his call to Behemoth, and while it was never said, she knew he wouldn't have been able to reach through to the Oblivion without her. This meant he needed her for his plan to be successful, which she had never considered devious until now. Something about the look on Lycus's face when she'd accidentally psychically shoved him was enough to give her pause regarding their whole relationship.

Alastor realized she very well may be but a pawn in Lycus's master plan and once achieved, she would become useless and be tossed aside. If this indeed was the case, which to her it was beginning to look like, she would not abide such treatment. She'd turn things around on Lycus before he'd even realized it happened, and by then it would be too late. The hurt Alastor felt fed her anger, and she spent the rest of the night in her mental box fuming while formulating a plan.

# PLENTY OF TIME TO DIE

LLOYD GRITTED HIS teeth and squeezed his rough, callused hands into fists. Fuck running. Whether or not Magoth was tasked with killing him, Lloyd was going to ring the little shit's neck before breathing his last. Just as he lunged forward to grab for him, Magoth leapt to the ground and Lloyd's momentum carried him into and over the railing. He landed hard enough on his back to knock the wind out of him, and as he struggled to suck air, the dwarf fell on his back as well having exploded into near seizure-inducing laughter.

Lloyd held his ribs with one arm and attempted to push himself up with the other, but barely made it halfway before collapsing. He paused, allowing his muscles to relax, and gulped down breaths as his diaphragm began to loosen its hold on his lungs. Now able to breathe, Lloyd pushed himself up into a seated position as Magoth approached, his laughing hysterics tapered off into a fiendish giggle. There was nothing he could do but stand his ground.

"Just get it over with, you little bastard!" Lloyd shouted.

"And what, pray tell, are you speaking of?"

Magoth sneered and Lloyd resented the playful attitude of the dwarf, given the dire consequences of the situation.

"If you're supposed to kill me, you can try, but I'm gonna take a piece of your ass with me."

Lloyd rose to his feet and towered over the short man, ready to unleash all hell upon him.

"Oh, Lloyd," Magoth sighed. "You *will* die soon enough, but not quite yet."

Lloyd took a quick glance down at the body of the Englishman, then narrowed his eyes at the game master.

"And what the hell does that mean?"

"It means, gunfighter, that you won this particular challenge. You won't be. .. exterminated until you've failed as previously stated in the rules. Make no mistake, you will fail, and you will die, only not this moment."

"So, what, I was supposed to shoot the English fella? That was the purpose of the game?"

"Bingo."

"And what if I'd chosen wrong? Who or what were behind those other doors?"

"You were."

"What? The hell ya' mean?"

Magoth leaned back against the post holding the railing, the glee Lloyd stripped him of having returned.

"I hated that limey fuck and Lycus wanted him taken care of anyway," Magoth said. "Quite frankly, I have to admit I was rooting for you on this one. In case you haven't realized, Cocytus doesn't follow the laws of time or space. Behind the other star-doors was a version of you in this exact moment pulling the trigger a split second before the you here with me could, thereby effectively killing yourself. It's quite entertaining when it happens that way, but as I said before, I'm glad it did not. *This time.*"

Lloyd reeled from the explanation, trying to wrap his mind around the concept of being killed by a version of himself and how close it came to happening. If he hadn't changed his mind at the last second, it would be him face down, leaking blood and brains into the thirsty desert sand. He didn't notice Magoth had already started walking to the next challenge until the dwarf called out to him.

"Don't dawdle Lloyd," he said. "There are plenty more chances for you to die left. It's only a matter of time."

The man cackled with laughter and Lloyd fumed as he turned to follow in its maddening wake.

# PLOTTING FOR CALAMITY

**SAMUEL AND PAIMON** stared down at Luke's corpse like they expected it to reanimate at any moment. They'd been on the outskirts of Lycus's property for over an hour, but neither had started to dig yet. Aside from Samuel asking Paimon to roll him a smoke, the two hadn't spoken a word since they left Lycus's house. The horses brayed and the two men shivered, though not because of the temperature, each waiting for the other to speak first. Surprisingly, it was Paimon who broke the heavy, settled silence.

"Was it just me," he started, "or did you think when he fell over like that it was part of his plan?"

Samuel bristled at first as if he'd taken offense, but calmed quickly, chuckling softly to himself.

"No, wasn't just you. I guess I was thinking the same thing."

The two shared a stifled laugh that tapered off into the vacuum-like silence of the night. Paimon removed his pouch and before Samuel could ask, he handed him one of the two smokes he'd proficiently rolled in a matter of seconds.

"You know," Samuel said, taking a drag. "I've been thinking maybe Luke was right."

"'Bout what?"

"'Bout everything. This job, this place, the so-called 'boss' up there on the hill calling the shots, calling *our* shots."

Paimon nodded along, puffing smoke like a manic steam engine set to overheat.

"Think about it," continued Samuel. "We never let anyone else tell us what to do or how to do it. *Never*. Then, all of a sudden, we wind up here and start taking orders from this Lycus fellow like desperate whores trying to make a last buck before closing time. That's not us, that's never been us, so how in the hell did it come to this? One second, we're the baddest bandits in the west, and the next we're takin' orders doing someone else's dirty work. And for what, some drink and women? We had all we could want *before* we came here."

Paimon rolled another smoke and continued to nod, but he wasn't just doing it to appease Samuel, he was actually thinking about what his now only partner was saying.

"I think Luke was right about this place. He was right about everything," Paimon said, lighting up his new smoke. "How did we come to be in Cocytus, anyway? Every time he would ask me about it, I thought I remembered, but now I'm not so sure. I know you said it was on account of us gettin lost in a sandstorm, but I can't even remember the last time there was a storm like that."

"I didn't really remember it that way," Samuel spat. "I just said it to shut Luke up. He always wanted to talk about it at the worst times, like when we would be about to eat or get a poke or two in before hitting the trail."

"Then how *did* we get here? Do you remember anything about it?"

"No. I don't even remember how long we've been in this crazy fuck of a place."

Samuel's tone was cold and flat. He was quiet for a few seconds, then started to pace before Luke's half-sacked body. He'd tried to recall the circumstances surrounding their arrival in Cocytus, he really had, but it always left him dizzy and lightheaded before the subsequent headache set it. Even when he tried to remember what the Three were doing just before they arrived in Cocytus, the result was the same.

"I reckon I can't remember either," Paimon said finally.

"All this time we've been distracted and manipulated by Lycus all the while believing we were working for him because we wanted to. Meanwhile, he's got us so under his thumb we don't know whether we're coming or going, and the worst part is we were okay with it. More than that, we're apparently happy to do whatever he tells us."

"I hadn't thought of it like that, but now that you say it, I think you're right."

"Of course, I am," Samuel was fuming now having worked himself up, "but Luke was right the whole time, and we should've been listening to him 'stead of worryin' 'bout getting our dicks wet or pouring liquor down our holes. Well, no more."

"What are you supposin' we do?"

"I say we show him who we really are. It's time to bring *true* Calamity to Cocytus."

Paimon exhaled and the dissipating smoke in front of his face revealed a sly smile the bandit hadn't worn in quite some time.

"Let's bury Luke then get to work," Samuel said, taking down of the shovels he'd tied to the side of his saddle. "First, help me get his boots off. I always wanted a pair just like 'em."

# PART II

# LYCUS'S LAMENT

BACK BEFORE THERE was Cocytus, before Texas, before anything, there was only Oblivion. It's been called different things by different groups of people throughout time, but it's all the same place. Although, it isn't really a *place,* at least not in the physical sense one might think. One way to describe it is like living in an eternal waking nightmare, but even that doesn't do justice.

Oblivion lies between physical planes of existence as a reality unto itself where the most deplorable things bear fruit that find its way into other worlds to corrupt and sow chaos. Wickedness is banished to Oblivion, but not bound there, and can easily slip back and forth between dimensional planes with ease. The entities dwelling there have been known as deities to some and devils to others. They've gone by different names at different times, but their objective remains the same.

Chaos. Destruction. Death.

Those native to the wretched realm are often referred to as 'Oblivionites', though no one knows where the term originated. After eons of moving back and forth between worlds inflicting their particular brand of damage, both physical and psychological, the beings of Oblivion discovered they could stir chaos in other realms by simply projecting their influence thereby conserving their own great power.

They found they were able to manipulate energy and lifeforms as they wished without leaving Oblivion, therefore allowing them to remain inaccessible and virtually invincible. While the amount of energy, strength, and sheer will to destroy an Oblivionite has not been found anywhere across all known existence, the longer they're away from home the weaker they become. Ending an Oblivionite completely is impossible, especially in a human-based world, but they can be weakened to the point of being dominated.

It wasn't something that happened often but there were few occasions in which arrogance had gotten the better of an Oblivionite without realizing how weak they'd let themselves become. While they can't be killed those captured wished for death as they'd be beaten mercilessly, thrown into underground dungeons and forgotten, or repeatedly burned and scattered.

Most of the fallen would be sought out and 'rescued' by fellow Oblivionites taken back home to recover their power, but not all were so lucky. Some were left to rot in the worlds they'd let themselves get stuck in for eternity or until the Universe itself ground them into dust on the cosmic winds. These were the lucky ones, but Lycus was not counted among them. The circumstances of his departure from home were wholly unique, specific only to him.

Hierarchy does not exist in Oblivion, and for good reason, but Lycus wanted to change that. He proposed wildly detailed plans of organizing into ranks beneath designated leaders presiding over certain territories of the realm. He wanted to structure Oblivion into a kind of militaristic machine where different branches and specialized squadrons would be deployed together to cause high levels of decimation regardless of the destination. Lycus wanted Oblivion to absorb the dominated realms fortifying their strength and tightening their hold on adjoining worlds now easily conquerable by their united, organized front.

His major oversight was Oblivionites were not

interested in being united or organized and never would be regardless of potential benefits. The very idea was the antithesis of Oblivion's existence, and the thought of not only making but following rules *while* taking orders from a designated 'better' induced confusion and anger. This wasn't chaos, it was control, and not a being in all of Oblivion wanted that. They would not allow it to happen. Lycus was trying to turn their quiet personal acts of destruction into strategic strikes carried out in groups already thinking two steps ahead to eliminate randomness from the equation.

There was no time wasted in expelling Lycus from Oblivion. They swarmed and overtook him quickly with ease, forcing him out into a random world where he would remain indefinitely. All entrances back into Oblivion were sealed off to Lycus through a magic he couldn't comprehend, but it didn't stop him from spending the first two-hundred and fifty years on the planet seeking out every single one of them until his worst fear was confirmed.

He'd been banished from Oblivion, banished from his home. He wasn't sure how or why it was possible, but after exhausting all resources, Lycus was forced to accept the truth. As tempted as he was to take his anger out by causing insurmountable destruction, he stayed his temper to save his strength. He couldn't stop his power from hemorrhaging, but could slow the process by *not* creating catastrophe on a grandiose scale.

It was difficult in the beginning, and he blew off more steam than he would've liked a time or two but got a hold on the issue. Lycus refocused the energy of his anger on finding a way to get back to Oblivion, and he lived in seclusion on an unsettled and otherwise unpopulated mountain range as he worked to crack the code. All inroads were cut off and sealed tight to keep not only him but anything else from getting through, but what vexed Lycus was he could still sense the presence of these scattered gates. His entire being acted as a divining rod in that he could feel his way across oceans to the location of these passages, could put his hand right up to where the opening lingered half in this world and half in his own, but could not pass through.

Lycus thought being able to sense but not enter the openings into Oblivion was another wrinkle of his punishment meant to leave him forever searching with endless disappointment. It wasn't until he approached the problem from a different perspective that Lycus realized he'd been wrong in assuming it was part of his punishment. It was an oversight. He'd been looking at the situation from one side for so long the solution leapt out once he changed his approach.

If Lycus could sense the gates, it meant they still existed, which in turn meant, while they didn't work for him; they still worked. Permanently sealing off the cross gaps to Oblivion would remove them completely leaving no way in or out from the world to which he'd been sent, but the fact the gates were still there meant they weren't closed completely. Just because Lycus couldn't go in didn't mean something else couldn't come out.

He'd discovered a flaw in the Oblivionites method of ensuring his unjustified excommunication was permanent, but even more, he knew just how to exploit it. The trouble was Lycus could no longer send communications into Oblivion, and even if he could, it didn't mean whoever came through would take him back with them.

He needed to think bigger. If he could no longer get to Oblivion, he would bring Oblivion to him, and that was when he thought of Behemoth. When it came to size on all accounts, there was none bigger than him, and Lycus could use the creature's tremendous mass to carry out his plan. He knew it would require a considerable amount of work to generate enough power to breach the seals and call out to the giant, and from that, Cocytus was formed.

Lycus used the bulk of his remaining power to manifest the town, knowing he'd be able to recoup that strength and more once the wheels of his plan were in motion. Cocytus was hidden within multiple endless layers of existence between Oblivion and the world unto which he'd been banished where it would serve as the staging area for his siege.

He'd need to lure people whose souls were heavy with apathy, selfishness, and greed. Men with egos too inflated to keep their giant heads up. The collective mass of sorrow would weigh down Cocytus until the arrival of Behemoth tipped the astral plane on its side to pull Oblivion through into the horrid world that was his prison. This was no easy feat and would've taken hundreds of thousands of years if Alastor hadn't entered the equation. The unexpected addition of her particular talents sped things up significantly, and Lycus's excitement grew along with his vigor.

With her help, he didn't need to wait centuries while his power slowly built back up, and within weeks was strong enough to reach directly through to Behemoth. He sent the call out through Alastor, who homed in on the beast pushing the message through to him. She acted as a cloaking device for the communication, disguising who was sending it and how. Lycus used the girl like a Trojan horse to get his message through the gates and straight to Behemoth. Now, the beast was coming, albeit slowly, but would soon reach Cocytus, bringing with it the morbid paradise Lycus called home.

The souls he'd lured to his manifested makeshift town had done the job of increasing the cosmic weight to the tipping point, and he was poised to rip through the fabric of reality like a rock through wet paper. There were a few straggling souls still plodding through the games of Cocytus, but he'd already reached his goal without them. They were of no consequence to Lycus now and would be ripped apart and vaporized with the coming of Oblivion along with all the souls he'd collected. The Calamity Three had been reduced to two, now hobbled by the loss of the man who held them together, and while he had reason to question Alastor's loyalty based on her behavior of late, he wasn't concerned. The girl wouldn't survive the merging of worlds, despite him leading her to believe she would not only live but rule at his side. No one and nothing could ever rule over the chaos that was Oblivion, but she didn't know that. Alastor was and had always been one of many disposable elements in Lycus's quest to return home.

He'd finally reached the apex and was now barreling down the other side of the hill. He was unstoppable. All he had left to do was sit back and enjoy as the elements from thousands of years of planning fell into place. The stories of old gods and the hubris that tore them asunder were only that, stories.

There would be no fall for Lycus, no melted wings of wax plunging him to earth, no hero arriving in the eleventh hour to stop him. There would be no redemption for the world in which he'd been imprisoned, nor would there be anyone left to mourn its passing.

# THAT DAMN HORSE

THE ARRANGEMENT BETWEEN Caroline and Cherub worked well and soon grew into more of a mother/son relationship rather than employee/employer. The boy learned fast and required little to no supervision in the garden once he'd been shown what to do, which left Caroline free time to continuously hone her natural craft. The entire first year Cherub worked for the woman, he would rise before the sun, walk the path to her cottage, then traipse back home when the day was coming to an end.

Of course, he'd learned early on the woman was a witch, but despite all he'd heard about them wasn't afraid. Besides, she wasn't the wrinkled hag he'd been led to believe witches were, and even if she had been he had no reason to pass judgement on the only person who'd shown him any affection in years.

Being a young man all alone, Cherub lacked the ability and know-how when it came to maintaining the home he'd been left with, and the dilapidated domicile fell quickly into further disrepair until it had all but crashed down around him. It took more time than she thought necessary, but Caroline eventually convinced the boy to live with her after a week of nasty thunderstorms punished the surrounding plains with non-stop rain in drops the size of English cannonballs. The resulting flash flood swept the broken-down small house across the property, where it smashed into the crumbling barn. The two structures collapsed into each other as a lumpy warped tangle of rotting wood and rusted nails mangling beyond recognition any and every memory Cherub had of the place.

The only shelter he had access to had been washed into a small creek that would dry out long before the wreckage could make it to the major river it fed into. He imagined somewhere miles downstream the pieces of the house were stuck in muddy banks having formed a terrifyingly mutated version of his home.

Cherub moved into a small shed behind Caroline's house she'd been surreptitiously converting into a room for him since their first meeting. She hoped keeping him close would allow her to somehow protect him from what was to come despite the invariable end she continued to see in spontaneous visions, which now included a black horse and a foreign pistol, though there was no context for them yet. Caroline didn't know where the sense of protection she felt for Cherub came from, but the strong feeling of urgency accompanying it reaffirmed she was doing the right thing. Their paths were meant to cross, and while the witch was to play a crucial role in their relationship, she didn't know exactly what it was yet.

Cherub worked even harder once he'd moved into the shed, which Caroline made into a dwelling he deemed fit for a king. It wasn't much, but after living in busted down squalor his whole life, it felt like a castle. As the years went on Cherub had taken to not only completing his assigned duties with strict care but also doing other work around the property without being asked. He put a whole new roof on the witch's cottage in a matter of two days and eventually raised a small barn after months of collecting supplies. It was smaller than the one in which he'd found his precious Colt but was constructed to be solid and sturdy unlike its predecessor.

Cherub never asked Slim about what happened to his mother, and he just plain didn't think about his father. He was still sharpening his talent as a gunfighter only now the pursuit had become something of his own, and not tethered to secondhand memories of a ghost he never knew. He'd gotten better than just good with his trusty Colt and continued to constantly improve without seeming to hit any form of a plateau. Cherub also taught himself how to care for his weapon, knowing as long as he took care of it, the gun would take care of him.

The boy had come across just about any issue one could have from his Colt Peacemaker and learned to remedy them because of it. Rusted firing pin? He could take care of that with a file and some elbow grease. Jammed cylinder? Cherub knew how to keep the mechanism oiled just right so it would never be an issue again. He'd taken it apart, cleaned every inch, and put the thing back together so many times he could do it blindfolded and sometimes did just to challenge himself. Cherub was a believer in being prepared for any situation he may find himself in as an expert gunfighter.

Occasionally, he would shoot other guns owned by the blacksmith in town, but never took to any of them. Cherub proved his skills to the smithy by winning a bet in which he'd been challenged to shoot three cans perched on a railing from ten paces. The wager came about when the man saw Cherub's pistol strapped to his hip, something he believed the boy had no business carrying in the first place let alone firing the thing, and he intended to prove it. When asked, Cherub proudly declared it was indeed his Colt, and he was, in fact, a crack-shot. The man nearly doubled over laughing and told Cherub if he could knock the three cans down using only three shots he'd buy the kid a year's worth of cartridges, but if he couldn't then he'd have to hand over his gun to the blacksmith.

Cherub didn't bat an eye at the challenge unaffected by the man's lack of faith in his ability, and instead decided to handicap himself further. The boy turned around and walked an additional twenty paces from the appointed target, which sent the man into a second fit of laughter.

"Okay, boy," the blacksmith shouted. "You can stand back there if you want, but you still only get three shots to knock them cans down. You understand?"

"I'll only need one," Cherub answered coldly.

"Did you say on—"

The man was cut off by the satisfying bark of Cherub's Colt and turned just in time to see the single shot collide with the bottom right corner of the can on the right sending it spiraling down the railing into the two other cans. They hit the dusty street, striking three succinct tinny notes ascending in the key of G. The man turned around to find Cherub next to him again, pistol holstered, and all he could think to say was, "Oh yeah? Do it again," and so he did. Cherub did it over and over, nailing every trick shot the man threw at him with minimal effort and zero ego.

The smithy, whose name was Magoth, took a liking to Cherub and by the end of the day the two were talking like they'd known each other all their lives despite being separated by many years. When asked about the unique moniker, the man said only that it was a family name with no further elaboration, so Cherub left it at that. The blacksmith kept good on his end of the bet and always had boxes of cartridges ready for the boy every time he and Caroline came into town. Cherub spent hours with Magoth while the witch shopped or had a drink or two at Slim's, and he learned a lot from the blacksmith. Outside of forging ploughheads, hatchets, and mounds of nails, Magoth made parts for damaged guns of which he'd amassed an impressive collection.

Cherub shot every single one of the weapons on several occasions but favored his Peacemaker over them all. Not even other Colt models held a candle to it in his eyes, and though he was just as good a shot with any gun he touched, none felt as right in his hand as the old Colt. Magoth had seen it before, the bond a gunfighter has with their own weapon, and completely understood the boy's reluctance toward change. Cherub wasn't arrogant about placing imaginary importance on his weapon to justify his predilection, he just knew what he liked, knew what worked for him, and kept the reasoning to himself.

Later that year on his fourteenth birthday Carolyne gave Cherub a Winchester rifle Magoth had completely rebuilt and even improved upon adding several custom adjustments. He gave it a hair-trigger for quick fire action and used pine for the stock to make it lighter. The rifle was guaranteed to shoot straight and true from two hundred yards and coupled with Cherub's talent could be used to make any long-range shot with ease. The weapon was so accurate, you'd almost have to try harder *not* to hit your target with it. The boy was grateful to receive the rifle and even excitedly rushed out back to put the blacksmith's specs to the test.

Neither Magoth nor Caroline witnessed Cherub shoot the Winchester again after that day, though he kept it cleaned and maintained just as well as he did his Colt. They knew how attached he was to the pistol and took no offense. There was an intangible magic at work when the boy and his gun were combined that superseded any advantage a specialized weapon had to offer. Neither the smithy nor the witch would've been the least bit surprised if Cherub told them he had a mind-meld with the Colt and used his thoughts to fire the thing, something Caroline already believed to be at least partially true.

Cherub eventually took on a part-time position helping the blacksmith two days a week, but he never fell behind on his work for Caroline. She'd done more for him than anyone and his job with her took priority over even his shooting practice as the boy wouldn't dare touch his weapon until his daily tasks were complete regardless of the amount of time it took. There were days Caroline insisted he go visit with Magoth, or spend the time shooting, but he was too disciplined and loyal to ever take her up on it.

Cherub took to blacksmithing almost as quickly as he'd

taken to shooting and excelled in the skill nearly as fast. Magoth started him at the bottom his first week having the boy haul loads of iron in and out of the shop, stoke the flames of the forge to keep up the intensity of the heat, and sand the wear from his many hammers before polishing them to shine like new. Cherub firmly grasped the art of manipulating metals and in no time was handling smaller tasks of Magoth's daily workload leaving more time for them both to make, fix, and shoot guns.

Shortly after turning sixteen Cherub was able to buy a horse, doing so completely on his own, without telling Caroline or even Magoth he'd been saving for one. He'd always been fiercely independent, accepting help only out of dire necessity and even then, begrudgingly. If the two of them knew he was planning to buy a horse, he figured they'd want to chip in or try to influence his decision, and this was something he wanted to do on his own. He had no idea the reaction, at least from Caroline, would've been the exact opposite, and had the witch known Cherub planned to buy a horse, she would've done everything in her power to stop him.

She'd had a bad feeling since she woke up that day but couldn't pin down what was nagging at her until she stepped out the front door of the cottage and saw Cherub coming up the path atop a young black mustang. The horse's coat was so dark it gave the animal an unsettlingly unreal appearance. A smile like she'd never seen the boy wear before stretched out his tight, stoic features to the point of appearing comically mutated.

Carolyne had seen the horse before in violent flashes from a premonition she wished to forget. It was a sign of the coming cataclysm she'd hoped to prevent. The witch choked back tears and waved to the boy, doing her best to reciprocate his smile without letting the terrifying despair show through. Carolyne knew things would start happening quickly now. They always did at the end.

# WITCHES COME HOME TO ROOST

**SOMETHING HAPPENED TO** Alastor after her unintentional confrontation with Lycus. She was troubled deeply by the realization, but acceptance came quickly after what she'd been shown while in the box. Their auras bumped up against each other as a result of her psychic outburst and she was granted access to a part of Lycus he'd successfully kept hidden her entire life. She didn't know whether she felt more anger or heartbreak over discovering her history, their relationship, and Lycus's intentions had all been predicated on lies.

Nothing she knew was true. Everything, all of it, had been conjured, manipulated, and planted in her mind. She wasn't supposed to know this, was never supposed to know, but on account of Lycus's shortsightedness when it came to how powerful she truly was, Alastor saw everything. He knew she'd get stronger but assumed he'd have no trouble controlling her through a false bond of loyalty. Lycus made himself out to be noble when he in fact was a scourge upon any plane in which he existed.

Alastor could see it all now laid out for her clear as crystal as she brooded within the box. She watched Lycus using her, keeping her under his thumb from when she was a child to the present, and even what the future held if she remained grafted to his influence. She saw him kidnap her from the coven to which she belonged. Watched him return to mercilessly slaughter the entire lot of witches upon realizing what he could achieve for himself by guiding the application of her powers.

As she took this information in, the safe space in Alastor's mind was invaded by a presence, or more accurately twenty-three different presences, but she was not disturbed by the intrusion. She couldn't see these visitors, even with her mind's eye, but felt the energy swirl around her, discerning it as the slain members of the coven, *her* coven. Lycus had no idea when he massacred the witches that night, he'd slit his own throat.

Alastor was born a witch and therefore imbued with the ability to develop strengths in certain areas of the craft, but the extraordinary awakening of power within the girl was not the result of an anomaly. The witches' spirits found a way to reach through to her from beyond, and now finally the opening was wide enough for them to save the coven's only surviving daughter while destroying the dark being who'd taken them away from her. A comforting warmth like she'd never known settled around Alastor before sinking into her body as a part of her. It was the first time she'd ever felt a sense of peace, of true purpose.

Every bit of contrived connection she had to Lycus was severed in that moment. She was no longer loyal to him, or Cocytus, or the Oblivion in which she'd been led to believe she'd reign. She had no allies in this, nor did she want any. Alastor no longer felt anxiety over meeting with Lycus in the morning as he'd requested. She was looking forward to it.

# WE'LL BE BACK, AND YOU'LL BE SORRY

**SAMUEL AND PAIMON** had been riding for what felt like hours, but time was hard to judge the longer you spent in Cocytus. The edge of town had been perpetually over the next ridge since they'd started out, yet they'd gotten no closer. Both men were aware of this strange wrinkle and had been for a while, but neither wanted to say anything, hoping the other would pipe up soon with a solution.

It was just as well for as good of a plan the two managed to cobble together, if it could be called a 'plan'. Samuel suggested they leave Cocytus, round up a posse of fellow bandits and outlaws, then come back to wreak havoc on Lycus and his precious town. Paimon nodded along like always, but neither of the men put any additional thought into the notion.

The Calamity Three worked alone exclusively and hadn't made many friends among fellow killers and criminals, so actually finding folks to join their self-serving so-called mission who didn't just shoot them where they stood would be difficult. Motivation was another issue in that they hadn't considered what to offer in way of compensation to make the prospect sound enticing. There was no honor or loyalty among thieves, and they wouldn't be compelled to help simply based on the plight of Samuel and Paimon. Bandits were not part of an over-arching fraternal order of brotherhood, and even when working in groups, it was an 'every man for himself' kind of occupation.

Another glaring oversight was if they were able to amass any semblance of a posse. They had no idea what to do once they got back to Cocytus with them. The Calamity Three worked like a well-oiled machine acting as a single-minded cohesive unit when unleashed upon their soon-to-be unfortunate victims, but there weren't three of them anymore. They'd been hobbled. Luke was a crucial part of their success and without him, Samuel and Paimon may as well be two hands trying to work without a head. The two of them equated to a horse with a busted leg that needed to be shot.

Over the time they'd spent essentially trotting in place, it sunk in with both of them just how much they needed Luke. Without him, they were tantamount to useless.

"Hold on, just hold on now," Samuel barked, pulling back on the reins.

Paimon did the same and stopped alongside his remaining partner. He stared off into the impossible reach of the never-ending horizon and rolled a fresh smoke.

"This ain't right. We both know it ain't."

"Yup," Paimon said, exhaling smoke that turned purple against the sky's reflection of darkness.

"I mean, look at it." Samuel gestured ahead. "The edge of town hasn't moved all night. We've been riding for hours and ain't gotten no closer!"

"Mm hmm." More nodding, more smoke.

"We done been in and outta this shit-town . . . dozens a times at least. More probably."

Samuel wasn't good with numbers and threw the estimate out, unsure of what a dozen even were save for having heard it used in the same way before. When Paimon didn't correct him or interject, he continued.

"We ain't never had this kind of trouble before with comin' or goin'. He doesn't want us to leave now, though. He won't let us."

"Who?" Paimon handed a fresh smoke over to Samuel before lighting a second one for himself. "Luke?"

"Luke? Luke's dead, you idiot." Samuel snatched the smoke and inhaled deeply, hoping Paimon's special blend would take the edge off quickly. He needed to calm himself. "I'm talkin' 'bout that snake-in-the-grass son-of-a-bitch, Lycus. We shoulda' listened to Luke."

It was beginning to become a mantra.

"Yep." Paimon paused and smoked. "We should've."

"I know we should've, I just said that!" Samuel exploded, giving the horses a slight scare, and they flinched and snorted in response.

His voice echoed despite being surrounded by wide open space with nothing for the sound to bounce back off. The two sat in silence while Samuel fumed and Paimon smoked.

"Fine," Samuel said. "If Lycus wants us to stay, we'll stay, but I aim to make that fucker sorry he ever brought us here."

Paimon narrowed his eyes and nodded in agreement. Samuel tugged the reins to turn his horse around, but then pulled back to keep the animal from moving forward.

"What in the hell?"

Paimon turned as well, and his face echoed the sentiment of Samuel's remark. Ten feet in front of them lay the mound of dirt where they buried Luke, and a hundred feet beyond was Lycus's house. The men had ridden all night yet somehow remained where they'd started, having never left the edge of the property. A small explosion of thunder sounded from the low-hanging dark clouds rolling in over Lycus's home, and lightning danced within the approaching storm like a snake in the bushes waiting for its prey to come within striking distance.

"Goddamn bastard."

Samuel growled the words, but the tone betrayed his true emotion. For the first time in a long time, he was afraid.

# AND THEN ALL HOPE WAS GONE

CAROLINE KNEW SHE'D failed in her attempt to steer Cherub from the fate she'd foreseen when he brought home the horse. When she saw his new gun, there was no doubt. The gun actually came before the horse, but she hadn't been made aware of it until recently. It was the result of something he and Magoth had been working on, which the two of them referred to as 'the project' whenever she'd been around. Then he brought it home to show her, and Carolyne's world crumbled for the second time in as many weeks.

"It's called a LeMat," Cherub said proudly, holding it out in front of him showing it off. "It's a very rare French weapon used by—"

"I know what it is." Caroline cut him off. Aware of her tone, she softened before continuing. "I mean, I've heard about this particular gun before, and you're right, it is rare to find one these days. Where did you get it?"

"Magoth and I restored it." Cherub was smiling like when he showed her the horse and she suppressed a shudder induced by his expression. "Well, that's not entirely true. We really built it more than restored it. Wasn't much of the thing to begin with 'cept for this strange double barrel. It caught my eye in a pile of scrap Magoth had behind the shop, and I pulled it out to take a closer look. He had no idea it was even in there."

Cherub pointed along the barrel, indicating the pistol's only original piece. The work they'd done was painstakingly seamless and to the untrained eye would appear as an original.

"See, this top one shoots cartridge bullets," Cherub continued, excited to tell Carolyne all about it. "And this bigger one beneath it, well, you can fire buckshot outta' there with a wide enough spread to cut a man in half."

The witch gasped, hoping the boy read it as shared excitement, but he was engrossed with the weapon in his hand and seemed not to notice. Caroline looked down at Cherub's hip and saw his holster was empty.

"Where's your Colt?"

He looked confused at first, as if coming out of a trance the LeMat had put him in and glanced down at his holster before bringing his eyes back up to the gun in his hand. He smiled wider.

"Oh yeah," he started. "Well, I've been thinkin' it might be time to hang up the ol' Peacemaker and give somethin' else a try for a change."

He proudly brandished the LeMat again before smoothly sliding it into his holster in one slick motion. Now she saw not only was the gun new, but the holster and belt as well. Carolyne hadn't seen Cherub without his Colt and belt since it'd been big enough to wrap around him twice. It had become a part of his personality and the quiet, humble dignity of it suited him. The one he wore now was garish and ostentatious in comparison, words she would never use to describe Cherub. Until now, perhaps.

"You like the belt?"

Cherub lifted his arms and spun around so she could see the whole thing. The entire length was lined with bullets, but not the kind he usually used, and the last three spaces along his right side were purposely bigger to hold shells of buckshot. The leather was dark brown, almost black, and shiny, unlike his old one, worn soft and tan with age. Carolyne did *not* like this belt.

"I love it," she said smiling. "How much of the money you earned from Magoth did you have to part with for it? Quite a bit by the looks of it, I'd say."

"Well, you're half right," he said. "Magoth's money was used, but not from wages paid to me. He gave it to me as sort-of a gift for workin' so hard, especially with building the LeMat."

Cherub patted his hip at the weapon's mention, and she cringed not caring if he noticed, which he again didn't. She hated the gun as much as she hated the belt. She hated knowing what they meant more. Suddenly, Caroline was struck by a troubling thought.

"Magoth," she said. "Did he *give* you the gun as well?"

"Practically," he said, patting the gun again. "He said I should have it since I was the one who found the barrels in the junk heap, but we both worked hard on her. Magoth spent nearly a week on the handle himself, carved it all by hand."

Cherub patted his hip. Again.

"I made him keep my last two weeks' pay, though. I appreciate his generosity, but a man's gotta earn his livin'. He used his time and resources, and it's only fair he be compensated. 'Least, that's what I told him. He said we'd talk about it later, but I ain't taken no pay for that time. This more than makes up for it."

Carolyne looked at the ceiling because if she saw him pat the gun one more time, she was going to scream.

"He even got me a heap of bullets for this thing. It takes a different kind of cartridge than the Colt does, but he got so many it don't look like I'll be runnin' short on ammo anytime soon."

"Where?" Carolyn said. "These bullets. Where did he get them?"

"I reckon they were delivered before I got there one day 'cause I didn't see him bring them in, but when the LeMat was finished, he opened this old trunk and it was full of them."

Cherub's arm moved to touch the LeMat, but Caroline grabbed his hand and pulled it to her face. The vision that flashed across her mind was brief, and she immediately dropped his hand and stepped back.

"Wh—what's the matter, Ms. Carolyne?"

The excitement he'd been absorbed in was gone as genuine concern rushed in to take its place. The witch hesitated for a moment, then rushed from the room to her study. She needed to check something before saying anything else.

"Ms. Caroline? Ms. Caroline, are you okay?"

The worry in his tone broke her heart, and she struggled to keep her voice from cracking as she replied, but the words came out ominously troubling.

"Yes, dear, just a moment."

She didn't need to search for the book. She knew exactly where it was on the shelf and pulled it down immediately. It was a demonology tome she hadn't looked at in some time but studied thoroughly upon first receiving the text. Something had bothered her about the blacksmith, but any time she tried to figure out why, she became distracted else or would forget entirely what she'd been thinking about and why. What Caroline saw when she'd touched Cherub's hand revealed why that was, but she needed to double-check. She had to be sure. She hoped she was wrong.

The witch opened the book on her desk and flipped furiously through the weathered pages until she found the name she was looking for: Magoth.

*Magoth is an infernal sub-prince from the darkest realm. A master of illusion, he is able to take any form but appears primarily as a dwarf or, in some cases, an elf. He hinders operations and manipulates people and situations for his gain. He clouds judgement and is a master of misdirection. He wields magic far more powerful than any earthly wizard or witch and is never to be trusted. Magoth is a cruel prankster and a liar.*

Caroline slammed the book closed wishing the impact could obliterate the words she'd just read erasing Magoth's existence entirely. Her frustration turned to anger, which she directed at herself for being fooled by the demon. Carolyne wasn't a novice at witchcraft and should've been able to tell a spell was being used to confuse her regarding his true identity, she should've been able to deflect it. Why the spell seemed to have been suddenly lifted only moments ago gave her more reason to worry.

"Ms. Caroline?"

Cherub was standing in the door behind her now, his voice having taken on the softer quality of the boy he was rather than the man he was becoming. She turned around, opened her mouth to speak, but instead stepped to the young man and hugged him tight. A few rogue tears squeezed from her ducts and chased each other down her cheek. He hugged her back tightly, unsure of what to say or do when someone you care about was in distress. He'd been hardened by having to grow up too fast, never learning how to handle emotional situations because he didn't have time to learn.

He wouldn't have made it this far if he stopped to cry every fifteen minutes over the hand life had dealt him, but it didn't mean he was unsympathetic. He never said it out loud, but Cherub cared deeply for the woman who essentially saved his life and was fiercely protective of her.

Caroline knew they wouldn't see Magoth again. He was already gone, which was why the spell of confusion he'd fogged her mind with had been lifted. In her brief vision moments ago she'd seen Magoth the blacksmith as they'd known him, a tall burly laborer with an unwavering smile and a good heart, suddenly mutate into a scowling pitiless dwarf. The smile remained but held a devious and unsettling quality on this new face.

The worst thing about it were the black orbs bulging from his head, his eyes. Vacant yet sinister, exuding death, and doling out a steady gaze of torment. Caroline hugged

Cherub tighter, letting her tears flow freely now. Peals of thunder began to roll in from the east, and she knew there was truly nothing left she could do. She'd already lost him.

# FOOL ME TWICE

LLOYD FELT LIKE every trick shot imaginable had been thrown at him in his time with Magoth, and he'd bested every last challenge. After the falling stars and shooting the Englishman, he'd managed to steadily work his way through the course and appeared as though he were reaching an end. Magoth didn't get as upset as he'd been earlier when Lloyd was advancing, but a detectable sense of unease boiled beneath the surface betraying his unebbing smile.

While each challenged carried the implication of mounting difficulty, they started to feel derivative to Lloyd like they were being used to kill time more than challenge his skills. The last few shots had been absurd and counterintuitive, and Lloyd was very curious as to what they seemed to be waiting for.

One of the shots involved two falcons Magoth produced from thin air, one black and one brown. When released, Lloyd was to keep his eyes on them as they flew roughly a hundred yards out and dove to the ground snatching something up in their beaks before returning to the sky. The 'something' was a pebble, but only one of the falcons actually picked it up while the other mimicked the action of doing so.

They would then fly off in separate directions to put some space between them before turning around to fly directly at one another. The one with the pebble would release it before the birds crossed and Lloyd's task was to shoot the tiny rock out of the sky before it hit the ground and of course only had one shot with which to do it. The *ping* sound of Lloyd's bullet hitting the tiny stone was soft and distant, but both he and Magoth knew he'd nailed the shot.

The next required him to lay on his stomach and shoot the flower off a cactus roughly thirty yards away, not far compared to the distances with which he'd contended already. The towering succulent's trunk was thick enough for a person to hug without their hands meeting around the other side, and he judged it to be twenty feet tall give or take since he was estimating from the ground on his stomach.

The cactus's four arms were of equally impressive girth. The lowest sprouted halfway up the trunk with the other three defiantly spaced above it exploding upward anxious to extend their prickly reach beyond the trunk's massive crown, but only one managed to accomplish the feat so far. The third arm up on the plant surpassed the highest point by six inches, partially obscuring his view of the top.

The catch of the challenge was the flower itself being located on the *other* side of the cactus facing away from him without revealing or alluding to its position. He was supposed to 'discern' the flower's location and shoot it through the cactus sight unseen.

"A true gunfighter doesn't need his eyes to tell him where to shoot all the time," Magoth had said to him. "A *real* gunfighter knows."

What Lloyd *knew* was Magoth was full of shit with his *see with your heart* type bullshit. Real gunfighters were gifted yes, but they were smart having to use their brain to calculate and adjust for any number of potential variables that may affect a shot in the fraction of a second before the trigger is pulled. There's no time to check in with what you're feeling in that particular moment lest you miss or end up dead.

Lloyd learned a lot from years of traipsing through the desert, including gaining an intimate knowledge of the varied terrain. He didn't know technical scientific names of plants or rock formations but could determine the region he was traveling through based on what they looked like. This was a common-looking desert cactus, one like the thousands of others he'd seen, but only at first glance.

Lloyd studied the succulent, still able to glean important information from his compromised position. The shades of green varied from the trunk to each arm and, though nearly imperceptible, he could see the difference. He traced the different shades up from the base which showed him how the water was being distributed through the oversized plant thereby acting as a road map of sorts leading him to the unseen target. The back arm may have been able to temporarily take the lead in the limbs' race to the sky, but the trunk was not to be outdone. It was hoarding the lion's share of available water using it to give a 'fuck you' to its own adversarial arms in the form of a single blooming flower.

Though he couldn't see it, Lloyd followed the water's path up the hulking desert plant to where the flower would've, *should've*, sprung. The area was blocked from his view by the cactus's own overachieving appendage. Having to take the shot while lying on the ground was more of an inconvenience than a challenge, and Lloyd propped himself on his elbows as he took aim. He lined the shot up instantly, effortlessly, his brain making the necessary finely tuned adjustments to ensure the barrel was in the right position when he fired.

The bullet struck the back arm of the cactus and exited the other side with a muted wet pop. Lloyd saw flower petals explode from the crown, flutter to the desert floor, and gather around the base of the plant. He pushed himself to his feet and smiled down at Magoth as he brushed the dust from his clothes, but the dwarf was already heading in the direction of the next challenge, waving for Lloyd to follow.

# ALL OF YOUR DREAMS WILL COME TRUE

"Move it, gunfighter," Magoth called over his shoulder. "We're almost there. You may actually have a shot at getting your precious LeMat back after all. No pun intended!"

Hearing the man say they were close to the end of the game sparked embers of anxious excitement in the pit of Lloyd's stomach which were promptly extinguished by the hideously grating bought of laughter expelled by the dwarf. While he could plainly see Magoth walking just ahead of him, the sound of laughter came at him from all sides.

# AWAKE AND COME

**THE CALL WAS** weak and quiet at first, but its strength and urgency had steadily increased since the start. Behemoth inhabited the deepest depths of Oblivion and controlled entire timelines from the perpetual waking-dream state in which he existed. His presence alone was enough to keep most Oblivionites away from his dwelling, though occasionally there were those arrogant enough to seek him out.

It was the same every time. They'd come asking for something with nothing to offer, seeking an alliance benefiting only them, and each was met with the same response. Behemoth crushed the offending entities breaking them down to a molecular level which was then scattered across Oblivion. They couldn't be killed of course, but it would take eons to reassemble themselves.

The call was something different, though. Behemoth was to be sought out not beckoned, and its persistence was as intriguing to the beast as it was enraging. He'd been able to push it deep into the background with other inconsequential white noise until it was impossible to ignore. Behemoth emerged from the formless dreamscape in which he tortured multiple generations seething from the disturbance as the call became as loud and clear as it'd ever been.

Even for a being powerful as he, Behemoth was compelled, unable to resist following the call despite the unclear nature of its message. It clouded his mind with images of mass destruction on an ethereal level, and while the anticipated outcome wasn't specified, the creature had already determined it. They were asking for destruction, and he would deliver it on an incomprehensible scale to the extent of disintegrating the entire plain to which he was being summoned. As Behemoth plunged through Oblivion chasing after the call, a deafening thunder followed after him.

# DESTINY STEPS IN

THE WITCH AND the boy stood in front of the empty blacksmith stall, and while he'd been struck dumbfounded, she hadn't been surprised. Caroline knew this was coming since the moment they'd met, only she didn't expect it to come so soon. Cherub was sixteen years old, and while mature beyond his years, he didn't deserve to have what was left of his mostly corrupted youth taken. The thought further hardened the bitterness she felt toward the situation already.

Unable to hide her emotions back in the study, Caroline broke down and told Cherub why she was so upset. She didn't give the specifics of the vision. She couldn't do that to him, but she told him in no uncertain terms he was in danger, and it didn't look good. He accepted the information, keeping his emotions in check until she told him who Magoth really was, and how she'd come to suddenly know the truth about him.

Visibly upset, Cherub demanded they ride into town that instant to confront the blacksmith together, and only insisted further when she told him he wouldn't be there. Now he was staring into an empty space between *The First Bank* and the mercantile shop, a space he'd spent months working in a blacksmith's shop that had vanished into thin air, and the severe seriousness of what Caroline told him began to sink in.

Cherub paced in the street kicking up dust and mumbling to himself while absently touching the LeMat on his hip. Carolyne stood by, watching silently. She knew what he'd decide to do. There was no telling him any different. A slow rumble rolled across the plane drawing her attention to the approaching storm as it announced its continued advancement toward Cochran. The clouds hung low and heavy like over-saturated sponges with the color and texture of a pile of cats; the kind deemed unlucky by superstition.

"I just don't understand why?" Cherub said. "Why is this happening? Why me?"

"That's because it doesn't make sense, not to us. This was set in motion long ago, and you're one of the pieces that fit in the tableau. You always have been."

"Is it because of what took most of the men in town? Does it have to do with what took my Pa? What did my mother used to call it? Coll-something? Call-something?"

"Culling," said Carolyne. "It was called the culling, and yes; that's a part of it, but a small part. There's more to it than you can really understand."

"Yeah? Try me!"

It was the first time he'd ever raised his voice to the woman, and it startled them both, but thankfully shattered the rising tension rising.

"I didn't—I didn't mean it like that," she started. "I wasn't suggesting *you* specifically weren't capable of understanding; nobody is. Our minds don't know how to work that way."

Caroline did her best to explain the illusion of time and existence of countless versions of not only their reality, but a multitude of others beyond their ability to perceive. He continued to pace while the witch spoke, nodding along like he understood, though she couldn't imagine he truly did.

"How long?" Cherub said after she'd finished her explanation. "How long did you know about this?"

He gestured emphatically around while Carolyne remained silent, lowering her head. Cherub stopped pacing, stood in front of the witch, and put his hands on her shoulders.

"How long did you know?"

He was shouting at her now, but she knew the boy had every right to be angry. She'd only been trying to help in keeping it from him, trying to change the unchangeable, but he wouldn't be able to see it that way. Once his emotions subsided, he may be able to view it from her perspective, but it wouldn't be anytime soon, and she wasn't sure there was enough time left for him to reach the realization.

The thunder came louder now, angrier. Irritatingly, dark clouds reached toward Cochran like long shadowy fingers, the tips just grazing the edge of the tiny Texas town. Cherub remained undistracted; teeth clenched, he stared angrily at Carolyne waiting for an answer. The rolling clap of thunder had all but fully decayed before she finally spoke.

"The whole time." She said the words softly, her eyes aimed at the dusty ground.

"The whole time? What do you mean by that?"

"I mean *the whole time*."

The witch's voice rose, and she looked up into Cherub's face. Carolyne's fingers curled inward, turning her hands into fists as she shook not out of anger, but fear.

"When we first met on the path to town," the witch continued, her voice softened. "I've known since then."

His face hardened into an expression she'd never seen on Cherub before, and she wondered if this was what his gunfighter father looked like. The fixed jaw and narrow eyes made the boy suddenly appear well beyond his sixteen years. Carolyne was becoming increasingly uncomfortable as Cherub's anger pronounced itself through his body language, and she realized this was a defining moment for him. He wasn't the skinny young boy with a belt wrapped twice around his thin waist carrying a pistol big as his leg while claiming to one day be known as one of the world's best gunfighters.

Cherub was a man now, albeit a young man, and whatever trace of boyhood left in him evaporated before her eyes. He was tall and his body had filled out with defined muscle built from all his time working for her and the phony blacksmith. The gun belt he wore fit like it was made for him because it was, and the holstered LeMat further legitimized him as an adult and the gunfighter he always said he would be. Caroline hadn't noticed the stubble on his chin and above his lip until now and wondered if she'd been purposely ignoring his onset maturity.

This Cherub was somehow different from the version of him she'd seen in her vision but not in a physical sense. It was his attitude, his presence. He radiated a fierce confidence she felt smash against her in invisible psychic waves, and for a moment she felt a smoldering ember of hope spark from within. Something *was* different and maybe that meant she hadn't failed to alter Cherub's doomed destiny, or maybe crippling denial was causing her to sense things that weren't there? She was too emotionally taxed at the moment to tell either way.

"Why—" Cherub's voice was shaky with anger. "Why didn't you tell me sooner? We coulda' done somethin' to stop it."

"I've tried!" Her voice raised now. "I've done nothing but try to stop it every day since then, but it's—no matter how hard we try—some things can't be changed. I've always known that, but it didn't stop me from still trying to do something."

Caroline quietly sobbed as a gust of wind from the incoming storm kicked up, blowing the tears across her face sideways. He wanted to turn his back on her, wanted to stay angry, but his heart wasn't so hardened that he could entirely shut her out. This was the woman who'd taken him in. She gave him all the help he needed without making it feel like he was a charity case. She'd given him a sense of worth and for this, he couldn't begrudge the woman for the decision she'd made. He trusted Caroline had his best interests at heart and stepped forward to embrace the witch pulling her close to shield against the strengthening wind.

"I'm . . . I'm sorry," she sobbed against his chest.

He said nothing, instead comforting the woman with his embrace a few moments more before pulling back. The two communicated with their eyes, Caroline already knowing what he was going to say.

"I *have* to do something," he said. "I have to try, and I'm not waiting for whatever this is to come and get me. I'm going after it. You know I have to."

The approaching wall of black clouds blotted the sun out, completely coloring Cochran in an unnatural shade of gray. The thunder came like an avalanche, this time startling the horses where they'd been tied in front of the mercantile. The two animals, Cherub's coal-black mustang and Caroline's faithful steed, brayed and shifted on their hooves nervously anticipating the weather.

"I know you do. I know."

Carolyne held out her open palm and a small ball of yellow light appeared, floating in the center, dim at first, but it brightened quickly. She took her hand away, and the sphere floated at eye-level between them.

"Follow this light," she said. "It will take you where you need to go."

Cherub stared in confused wonder at the sphere as it rose into the air, glowing bright like a mini sun against the personified doom of storm clouds. He looked at Caroline and went to speak, but the witch cut him off.

"Go," she said. "Just go."

Cherub hesitated, lingering in the moment, but Carolyne's eyes further insisted on his immediate departure. He hurried over to untie his horse and leapt up into the saddle. The yellow ball of light bobbed for a moment in front of him before beginning to briskly move toward where the desert met the edge of town. He looked at Carolyne one more time, nodded in appreciation, and snapped the reins. The black mustang launched after the light and quickly worked up to a full gallop to close the distance.

The wind blew again, this time howling through the streets of town, and Caroline hugged her arms to her chest as she watched Cherub ride away. The boy and his horse were all but a silhouette on the horizon when the ball of light grew to the size of a train car and dropped down swallowing both horse and rider into its pulsing glow. The ball slowly shrunk to the size of a lightning bug before there was nothing left of it at all.

The ball, the horse, and the boy were gone, and Caroline knew she'd never see Cherub again.

# BEHEMOTH COMES

**LYCUS SAT AT** the giant desk, his chair turned around, facing the large window behind him. The perpetual dark was growing darker as storm clouds raced across the usurping all available space. He stared out at the dusty desert plain of a town he'd conjured from nothing, leaned back, and smiled, folding his hands across his lap. He had good reason for his onset jubilation, which erased the anger and anxiety he'd been experiencing recently. Lycus even pushed his conflict with Alastor far into the background of his mind after becoming aware several hours ago of something deserving of his entire mindshare.

She didn't matter anymore, and neither did confronting her about her abilities or what she may or may not be keeping from him. He couldn't care less what secrets the girl had since she'd suddenly become of no consequence to him. She'd served her purpose, and he didn't need her anymore. Unfortunately for Lycus, Alastor did not feel the same way and was presently stirring in her room across the hall as her consciousness emerged from the box in her mind. She'd learned the truth about Lycus, where she'd come from, and what she'd been used for. The powerful young mute intended to make him pay dearly for what he'd done to her and all the other poor souls she'd helped drag here to be forever doomed in the cursed town.

Lycus watched lightning dance across slate-colored storm clouds rolling in from the east, and the brief flash revealed silhouettes of Samuel and Paimon atop their horses standing at the edge of property where they'd buried Luke in the middle of the night. He knew they'd tried to leave town but couldn't, knew they'd be planning to come back after him, but it would be too little too late. Thunder roared concussively from the sky, and Lycus smiled even wider as the house shook with tremendous vibrations. Lycus knew what the storm signified. He was coming.

Behemoth was coming to Cocytus.

In the distance lightning raced to the desert floor striking random patches of sand, the heat instantly transforming the loose granules to pieces of glass. Lycus sensed Alastor was awake now and could feel the contempt for him she'd developed overnight, although he still wasn't entirely sure why. She couldn't hide everything though, and he knew she was coming for him, saw what she intended to do. The anger and hatred within her were palpable and intense to the extent it nearly manifested physically, and there was still a chance it would do just that.

Lycus wasn't the only one with a keen power of perception, and Alastor exploited the ability controlling exactly what he was 'sensing' from her. It was as if she'd installed a mental colander allowing only information she wanted him to have pass through the self-imposed filter. Alastor also knew Behemoth was coming because she'd called him. Lycus leaving an open line of communication between her and the beast unmonitored was perhaps his biggest mistake, but until last night he had no reason not to trust her. As far as he knew, she'd been sending out the call to Behemoth, gently luring him to Cocytus so Lycus could exact revenge while regaining access to his home.

From inside the box in her mind, Alastor was able to amplify her call, making it ring loud and clear in the creature's head, but it was not the same message she'd been sending prior. Behemoth was coming, and not for the reasons Lycus intended. She heard the thunder as she dressed, felt it vibrate through the house. The curtains were drawn, but the lightning was bright enough to pierce the thick fabric, momentarily casting a dull glow across the room.

Despite the cauldron of emotions threatening to bubble over, Alastor was surprised at how calm she was. This wasn't about just her, the childhood she didn't get, the life she'd never have. It was about the family she never got to meet. They'd been slaughtered so she could be used to help their killer go on to do far worse to many others with no regard for anyone but himself. Alastor knew what happened to the coven wasn't her fault, but she felt a powerful need to avenge them, to remember them.

She was ready now, stepped out into the hall, and approached the door to Lycus's quarters. It opened on its own and she walked through with a confident stride, knowing she was no longer under Lycus's thumb. He wanted to know what she was truly capable of, and Alastor intended to show him.

# HOLE IN ONE . . . HAND.

LLOYD SQUINTED UP at the sky.

"Are you sure that's where you wanna stand?" Asked Magoth, his edgy smugness having reached full bore.

Lloyd gave a slight nod with his chin but didn't take his eyes off the sky, knowing the dwarf was trying to distract him. He was standing in the spot, of that he was almost certain, but he needed to catch a glimpse of the bullet if he was going to catch it, which was the goal of this particular challenge. Magoth explained Lloyd was to fire a pistol straight up into the sky and catch the bullet in his hand on the way down before it hit the ground. The gun assigned to him for the task was an Enfield MK 1, a British manufactured weapon designed for their army's infantry men.

Lloyd had used this model of gun before but was by no means his favorite. It was known to jam, and the hinge beneath the cylinder had a pesky habit of locking up, making it impossible to load in a hurry. The good thing about the gun when it came to this challenge was it only had a range of sixty to eighty feet, which he hoped would make the bullet easier to see, but it also meant he wouldn't have a lot of time to locate and catch the thing.

"I don't know," chided Magoth. "Maybe you should move a little to the left. No, right! Right!"

Lloyd was unfazed by the attempt to split his focus and scanned the sky for the small hunk of lead. Dark clouds had started closing in around the gun range from all sides, but the thunder sounded like the storm was still a good distance away.

Lloyd used the contrast of clouds against the sky to his advantage and a moment later had the falling bullet in his sight. He put his hand out to line his palm with the falling slug, but the clouds shifted suddenly, and he lost it. His eyes darted frantically around, but the small dark spot he'd been tracking seemed to have vanished. He heard Magoth's snide chuckle, and for a moment Lloyd thought he might be licked until jagged lightning crisscrossed the sky. Against the momentary burst of brightness, Lloyd located the bullet's position, and moved his palm two inches to the left just before it struck.

He looked down at his hand, but instead of the fallen slug there was a slippery, red, wet hole. His brain figured out what happened a second before registering the pain, and Lloyd couldn't believe how foolish he'd been. He was so intent on finishing the games and getting his LeMat, he didn't think about the danger of catching a bullet in his hand, and it went right through the callused meat of his palm. The pain was excruciating but Lloyd did his best to compartmentalized it thinking two thoughts: at least it wasn't his shooting hand, and technically he'd won.

He held his damaged hand up and looked through the hole at the now hysterically laughing dwarf while blood poured freely down his wrist and arm to his elbow.

"Oh Lloyd," Magoth managed between chortling belly laughs. "For a second there, I didn't think you were gonna fall for that one."

The Enfield hit the sand with a muted thump as he instinctively went to clutch his wound with his good hand, but the prickly stinging pain made him let go.

"You little son-of-a-bitch."

Lloyd growled through clenched teeth and pulled the dusty bandana from his neck to tie around his hand and stop the bleeding. He used his teeth pull the knot tight, and the pressure forced torn raw nerve endings into each other producing a level of pain he'd not experienced. He would've passed out under the intensity of the sensation if not for his drive to kill Magoth.

He lunged at the dwarf, grabbed him around the neck and, ignoring the pain in his hand, began to squeeze channeling every ounce of strength his body had left into forcing the life out of the bothersome pest. Lloyd lifted the dwarf from his feet, tightening his grasp even more, but the only change in Magoth's face was the color turning from red to purple. The smile Lloyd had come to loath remained unaffected. The small man didn't even struggle, letting his arms hang slack at his sides as his legs dangled motionless.

Tiny red spots appeared in the whites of Magoth's eyes as the blood vessels began hemorrhaging, and while Lloyd preferred to use his gun for dispatching enemies, he'd had his hands around a neck or two before. He knew the small red dots meant his deed was nearly done and squeezed even harder, gaining strength through adrenaline-fueled rage. Suddenly, Magoth lifted his left arm and pointed, and Lloyd couldn't help but look over at what the dwarf was indicating.

His grip slackened, and Magoth hit the ground hard, gasping immediately for air. Twenty feet ahead, another challenge materialized: the final challenge. Lloyd knew this because painted on a wooden sign hanging from the post in front of them was a picture of his LeMat.

"See—see," Magoth managed between hacking attempts at gasping air. "See . . . we're near the end, gunfighter."

Lloyd glanced at the small man on the ground, contempt boiling behind his eyes, then back to the sign ahead.

"Too bad the fun ends here as well." Magoth attempted to laugh but could only cough instead.

Lloyd stepped over to the dwarf and kicked him hard in his ribs with the tip of his boot before beginning his walk to the final challenge.

# HOLE IN THE SKY

"ITS TOO LATE."

His back was to Alastor as she entered the deceptively large quarters, and the hard angles of the room framed her in sharp-edged shadows as she approached. He spun in his chair to face her, and a flash of lightning flooded the room, imitating daylight. It lasted less than a second, but in that moment Lycus saw the change in Alastor's eyes, and he knew she knew. He didn't know how, but it didn't matter.

"So, you know the truth, do you?" Lycus's gravelly voice dipped into a sinister octave. "Like I said, it's too late. Too late to avenge the witches I stole you from, too late to change what I've already used you for, and it's too late to attempt what I assure you would be an ill-fated attack upon me."

Alastor continued her advancement, and Lycus stood. He slammed his fist on the desk hard, causing the entire room to shudder, but Alastor remained steady on her feet, determined in her stride. She reached the desk and stopped as Lycus glowered down at her. He thought he knew it all, just like always, but this time, she had the upper hand.

"You can't stop me, child!" His voice boomed throughout the chamber, the echo refusing to decay. He pointed out the window behind him at the two bandits working their way across the property to the house. "They can't stop me either. It's already finished. Behemoth comes and with him, Oblivion will be brought to me."

Alastor lowered the bandana she kept her mouth covered with and smiled, something she'd not done much in her life until now. The foreign expression momentarily disarmed Lycus before further fueling his mounting anger. He'd expected her to make a move, attacking him in some way, but the confident smugness in her expression turned out to be worse. He put his hands down on the desk and leaned over.

"What's so funny?" His voice was a whispery growl. "I hope you realize you're not as clever as you thi—"

A deafening rolling thunder exploded directly over the house like a hundred bundles of dynamite shaking it with enough force to have cracked it down the middle had it not been fortified by Lycus's dark sorcery. Then, the sky above them opened up.

# ARRIVAL/DEPARTURE

**SAMUEL AND PAIMON** were in a full gallop when streaks of pink and green light began to swirl in the clouds over Lycus's home, and they pulled back hard on the reins bringing their devilish steeds to a halt. Guns in hand, ready to go in blasting, they holstered the weapons, realizing suddenly they were useless in this moment. The bandits exchanged a quick glance before returning their focus to the sky. The lightning was coming in quick bursts creating a strobe effect above the house, and the clouds transformed into something wet and sticky like melting taffy.

The edge of the widening circle turned a sickly green and began to spin as well, only in the opposite direction. Stunned by its disorienting effect, Samuel and Paimon were unable to look away.

"Whatcha' reckon we do?"

Paimon managed to holler the question between claps of thunder, but Samuel's gaze remained fixed on the sky until he repeated the question yelling louder this time. Samuel turned, went to answer, but was cut off by a dozen claps of thunder sounding in succession. It reminded Paimon of when miners blast the side of a mountain open to scrape out the valuable innards. He reached for his pouch and two seconds later was inserting a newly rolled smoke between his lips, but he didn't have a chance to light it.

As Paimon struck a match on his saddle horn and brought the flame up to his face, it happened.

The wind.

Wind, something forever absent in Cocytus, roared from behind the bandits ripping the smoke from his mouth and taking away any loose articles not attached to their saddles. They managed to hold their hats tight to their heads as the tremendous gust blew through them and up into the vacuum of the swirling opening. As suddenly as it came on, the wind stopped, and for a moment, all was silent. The thunder stopped, the lightning ceased, and even Samuel and Paimon held their breath without realizing they were doing so.

The rumbling came next, approaching at breakneck speed and growing louder the closer it got. The noise seemed to come from all around them and they swung their heads on their necks trying to pinpoint the exact direction until they realized together it was coming from above.

The ground shook, and the spooked horses bucked and reared back, throwing both men to the ground before sprinting off in the opposite direction. Samuel hit his head hard but remained conscious, and Paimon was pretty sure he'd broken at least one rib, but their pain was secondary to what they were witnessing.

Purple lightning fell from the center of the opening in quick bursts like striking vipers, electrifying the earth around the house. Cracks spider-webbed out across the dusty ground toward the ostentatious structure glowing the same purple shade. The rolling thunder reached its apex, and an ear-piercing cry came from the sky like vocalized terror played across a bed of amplified death rattles.

From the center of the circle in the sky, Samuel and Paimon saw the open-mouthed shrieking creature that was Behemoth. The gaping maw of the beast was unnaturally lined with vibrating pyramid-shaped teeth, and a forked tongue hung from the side of its mouth slithering like a thousand writhing boa constrictors. A single eye in the center of its head glowed the same shade of purple as the lightning and was flanked by two black horns jutting up like pointy onyx mountains. The beast's body was covered in scales that shimmered purple and gold as the knotted bulk of musculature composing its hulking frame quivered beneath.

The bandits watched in terrified awe as Behemoth fell from the sky, swallowed Lycus's house whole, and continued through the ground disappearing into the massive crater left in its wake.

# LIGHT AND DEATH

**CHERUB WAS MOMENTARILY** disoriented when the ball of light transported him to an unfamiliar place. He slowed his horse to a trot, then stopped, completely taking in the surroundings while trying to get his bearings. The air crackled, and the hair the back of his neck sprung erect, pulling the skin tight as the magic energy faded into the desert air. The hair on his arms was singed and he smelled it burning, an unfortunate but mildly annoying price to pay for traveling by way of magical conveyance. The yellow ball of light floating in front of him shrunk until it was gone.

Cherub ran his hand along the horse's neck, petting its mane, whispering to the animal in a soothing tone to calm it down, though the act was more for his own benefit. He looked around the surrounding desert, confirming he was not in Cochran anymore. Behind him was wide-open flat desert as far as he could see with no sign of the town he'd grown up in or the woman who'd sent him off to die. Aside from scattered cactus and a few large rocks, it was the same on all sides.

It appeared as though he'd been dropped in the middle of nowhere, and with the light ball he was supposed to follow gone, he had no clue in which way to go. He wasn't sure he was even facing the same direction he'd been when he arrived seconds earlier. An eerie vibe slowly tightened around Cherub, and he did not like whatever this place was. It looked like it could be any patch of desert between towns but looks were deceiving. It felt cold and detached, removed from the reality he'd existed in until moments ago.

Thunder came from behind and he spun around, surprised by the dark clouds moving quickly across the sky despite there being no wind to propel them. They devoured the clear night, leaving no part untouched by their dreary takeover. Cherub felt an odd sensation that something had changed, compelling him to take another look around. Straight ahead and quite a far piece away was something that had not been there moments ago, two somethings.

He knew it wasn't cactus or any other type of desert plant life, and easily recognized what he was seeing as the silhouettes of two people, one being considerably shorter than the other. Any other time he would've thought it was a person and their child, but the gut-feeling he had about this place told him otherwise as he snapped the reins, sending him and his horse galloping in their direction.

Lloyd thought his eyes were playing tricks on him when he saw the cloud of dust being kicked up by what looked like a horse and rider heading towards them. Heavy black clouds covered the entire sky now, and the gaps between claps of thunder were getting shorter with the storm's approach. He squinted out into the desert and, while it was still a ways off, confirmed the unmistakable shape of a man on a horse coming at them. He looked down, surprised to find Magoth standing at his side, having fully recovered from nearly being choked to death. He was smiling, of course.

"What's this all about?" Lloyd asked. "Is this a friend of yours or something?"

"Not really a friend of mine," Magoth chuckled. "Although, you may know him a little better than I."

"The hell's that supposed to mean?"

"That's not really important at the moment, but what *is* important is getting your LeMat back, right?"

"You know damn well it is," spat Lloyd.

"Well, the man who has it is riding toward us right now, and if you want it back, all you have to do is take it from him."

Magoth reached behind his back and produced an old beat-up Colt Peacemaker, which he handed up to the gunfighter. Lloyd had shot and handled many weapons, not only in his lifetime but also over the past few hours of playing this demented game, and he didn't recognize it as the same one he'd put away in the barn all those years ago.

"What do you say, gunfighter?" The dwarf grinned as his dark countenance dimmed further. "One shot and it's all yours."

# OPEN UP

**THE SOUND WAS DEAFENING**, and everything happened so quickly Lycus had no time to react when the ceiling came crashing down on him. Alastor, on the other hand, knew exactly what was coming and projected a psychic shield around herself as the house began to crumble. When the structure fell into the earth, the two of them fell with it. Being inside the mouth of Behemoth covered all the windows, making it impossible for Lycus to see what was happening, but he could sense it.

"What have you done, child?"

Lycus leapt across the desk at her, but it was too late. Crossbeams, wood and brick rained down between them, blocking him from his wayward protégé, as well as pinning him to the desktop. With the kind of strength Lycus possessed, he would've easily been able to lift the debris and continue after Alastor, but it was too much too fast stunning the displaced Oblivionite before he was able to act.

A chaotic cacophony swirled around him in a mixture of explosive thunder, crackling electricity, and snapping planks of lumber along with the distinct deafening shriek of Behemoth. A rumbling vibration came from beneath as the creature continued to plunge through the ground, taking Lycus, Alastor, and the house with it.

Minutes earlier, he'd been on the verge of celebrating the arrival of the beast and his return to Oblivion, and now he was trapped and falling. This was not how it was supposed to go. Something was wrong. He didn't know how she'd done it, but Alastor had ruined his plan, changed something crucial in her communication with Behemoth, altered something with the weight of his collected souls. Eons of planning and work seemingly gone in a matter of seconds on the whim of a little girl.

Lycus opened his mouth to scream, and it didn't matter that no sound came out because no one was there to hear.

# NO MORE GAMES

LLOYD HELD THE Peacemaker at his side, eyes fixed on the man who had his LeMat, waiting for him to get closer. The man's black mustang was quite the sprinter and used its speed to close the gap between them with its impressive speed.

"I may have to take that horse from the son-of-a-bitch as well," Lloyd said out loud, mostly to himself.

"I think you should do just that," Magoth said. "After all, *if* you win, you'll need a horse like that to hightail it out of town."

"Shut up," Lloyd said.

It seemed odd to Lloyd that this would be his final challenge. Hitting a moving target was easy. First day amateur stuff when it came to gun fighting. He kept his eye on the man with his LeMat but remained aware of his surroundings. Lloyd raised the Colt, taking aim, but thought there had to be something else to this challenge. It couldn't be this simple.

He was right, it wouldn't be.

Cherub could see the taller of the two people had a gun pointed at him. He was too far to tell the make of the weapon and therefore couldn't gauge what kind of range it had. He knew enough to know the man with the gun did not have his best interests at heart and could tell from his stance he aimed to shoot to kill.

He hadn't had the rebuilt LeMat long, but it'd been finished for a couple of weeks before Cherub showed it to Caroline, and in that time, he'd been practicing incessantly. Shooting the LeMat came easily to Cherub like any weapon he touched, but he'd become more than adept with the French-made gun in a short period. He'd even mastered taking into account the smaller, lighter bullets it fired.

Cherub could judge distance on sight and knew exactly where the invisible line in the sand he needed to cross was before he'd be close enough to hit his target accurately if a bullet didn't find him first. He focused on the rhythm of his horse's hooves striking the earth to clear his mind, as he was fast approaching the point his weapon would be of service to him against what was more than just a potential threat.

Cherub held the reins in his right hand as his left smoothly shifted down to his hip, hovering above the LeMat in a precise practiced motion as he prepared to draw.

What began as a soft chuckle from Magoth quickly evolved into laughter, but Lloyd blocked it out. His target was close enough for him to hear the steady beat of the horse's footfalls, and he focused on the rhythm to clear his mind. Lloyd held the old Colt steady, aimed at the man who had his gun, his LeMat, waiting for the rider to reach the weapon's range.

In those few moments, thoughts of Cochran flashed through his head. His wife. His son. A pang of guilt and regret came from the memory and for the first time in as long as he could remember, Lloyd wanted to be home more than anything and as soon as he took his gun back from this son-of-a-bitch, he was going straight back there.

Hammer cocked, he remained patient and calm, watching the man get closer, waiting, and when the rider was in range, his face came into focus. Lloyd didn't immediately recognize him, but was struck with a sense of familiarity. He figured it would be à propos for Magoth or whoever was running this 'game' to bring back one of his old enemies or even a former partner for this final challenge to give him pause, play with his mind. Perhaps it was a last-ditch ploy to trip him up at the finish line, but Lloyd wouldn't be thrown so easily. He steeled himself against this attempted distraction until he saw the man's eyes.

There was something else there, a familiarity that didn't come from friend or foe, but something much deeper. Like having déjà vu or being struck with the sudden memory of a past life. The way the rider's jaw was cut, the way his nose was pronounced, the way his glare was fixed, these features were recognizable to Lloyd because they were his own. This wasn't an acquaintance, a friend, or an enemy. This was family.

"Charlie?"

It all became clear the instant Lloyd said the name out loud. He didn't know how or why, but the man charging toward him was his son. It felt like he'd only been gone from Cochran for a day or so, and when he'd left, Cherub was just a boy who'd barely learned to walk. Now, somehow, his son was grown. He was a man. It made no sense, but nothing had since he'd come to this godforsaken town. He wasn't going to shoot his own son. He couldn't, but it was too late.

Lloyd went to lower the gun but realized he'd already pulled the trigger.

Cherub snatched the LeMat from his holster and began to fall backward as he lifted it. He felt pressure in his chest before he felt pain and couldn't understand why his arm wouldn't go any higher. He kept falling back until he was out of the saddle, tumbling head over heels to the hard, dusty ground. Taking a spill like that would've hurt a lot more had he not already been shot in the chest. Pain from his broken bones and bruised organs barely registered against the explosion of agony caused by the bullet shot from his own Colt.

It was the gun he'd carried for years, the one he'd practiced with, used to hone his craft and sharpen his talent. Yet, he'd quickly tossed it aside for the LeMat he clutched uselessly in a hand he could no longer feel. It was akin to the literal sting of a jealous lover and just as deadly. Cherub didn't know the man who'd pulled the trigger was the gun's original owner, an added layer of irony that would unfortunately be wasted on him but not Lloyd.

The mustang slowed nearly to a stop when something it saw beyond the two men spooked the horse into a fit rearing back on its hind legs. Lloyd spun, looking first down at Magoth, who was staring wide-eyed and slack-jawed at what had scared the horse. Off in the distance, a section of clouds spun in the sky with bursts of purple and green weaved around a growing aperture. Explosive thunder like colliding locomotives was followed by a piercing shriek like the wail of a thousand tortured banshees.

A wide-open mouth lined with the fangs you'd expect to see in a child's exaggerated drawing, too big for the space holding them, too sharp to be practical, broke the clouds first. Lloyd could only watch as the monstrous giant beast the mouth was attached to dropped from the sky and crashed into the earth, face first.

He shielded his eyes against the tremendous flash of light that followed the impact, and when he looked back, Magoth had vanished.

# WELCOME HOME

**NESTLED WITHIN THE** bowels of Oblivion the monstrous Old One settled into a deep slumber where from his perpetual dream state he spread destruction and chaos across infinite realms. He'd hardly been gone a moment, but for the worlds he tortured the absence equated to years spreading a false hope Behemoth would take great pleasure in crushing.

Lycus was trapped inside the creature, unable to move or speak while remaining completely aware of what was happening. His plan to bring Oblivion to him had failed, but he was back all the same. The ultimate double-crosser had been double-crossed and while in a sense he'd gotten what he wanted, there was no victory in it, and he'd garner no joy. He'd wanted nothing more than to return to Oblivion while exacting his revenge in one swift motion, and while he had returned, the vengeance taken was not his. It'd been turned back onto him, coming at his expense.

He'd been bested by Alastor, a child.

Lycus knew there'd be an eventual end to his current plight, albeit not anytime soon. It would take hundreds of thousands of years for his form to be broken down and dissolved by Behemoth, digested if you will, and his stripped particles would be expelled in all directions of the endless void. After an indeterminate number of millions of millennia, he'd eventually begin to pull together every cell, atom, and electrical charge that had made him up until fully regaining physicality. He would have her then.

Lycus didn't know what happened to Alastor, but he knew she wasn't dead or trapped like he was. She was out there somewhere, and he would scour the planes of existence one by one to find her once he'd been restored. He'd have to wait, but he was patient. His day would come. Again.

Alastor sat perched on the sleeping giant's shoulder, marveling at the sprawl of eternal nothing surrounding them. Lycus was right about her surviving, but he had no idea how close she actually was. Sitting in the void with the monster gave her a certain peace she'd not realized was possible. She felt neither rushed, nor particularly motivated to leave. Alastor didn't know how long she'd stay with Behemoth in Oblivion, but she was in no hurry.

With the help of the power imbued by her fallen coven, she'd easily deconstructed the intended plan manipulating her communication with Behemoth. She set the monster on Lycus and released the bounty of souls he'd collected as the creature broke the barrier to Cocytus. There was nothing left to ride Behemoth's drift in order to capsize one reality and yank it into another, and so he passed through taking only Lycus, Alastor and the house with him. The few Oblivionites still residing in the town such as Magoth were obliterated into ash when Behemoth passed through, becoming sand in the endless desert surrounding Cocytus.

Half of the freed souls passed through to be reborn into new lives in other realms, while the other half remained stuck in Cocytus with no memory of how they came to be there, or the life they had before.

Maybe one day Alastor would return to Cocytus to see what it's become, or maybe she wouldn't. For now, she felt most at home on the shoulder of a sleeping destroyer of worlds. Her bandana was pulled up over the lower half of her face like usual, but the smile hadn't gone away.

# LIKE FATHER, LIKE SON

MAGOTH NEVER REAPPEARED, so Lloyd was given no explanation as to what transpired, but he didn't need one. He walked out to the fallen man he somehow knew was his grown son, while chaos swirled in the sky behind him. He didn't know what was happening, nor did he care. Had he really been taken from his home and dragged here to play games and kill his own son? Yes, he had. Lloyd knew it was true as he stood over his fallen flesh and blood looking down into eyes that could've easily been his twenty years earlier.

Lloyd crouched next to Cherub's body and closed the boy's dead eyes before pulling the LeMat from fingers already gone cold. He stood, looked his weapon up and down, and returned it to the holster on his hip. It felt good to have it back. He felt complete again. Lloyd had calmed the horse and found a small shovel in the bedroll tied to the saddle. While massive plumes of dust settled in the background behind him, he dug a hole and buried his son. The gun range was gone now and there were no sticks or rocks around to use as a marker, so Lloyd stuck the Colt Peacemaker barrel down into the earth and left it there.

He mounted the black mustang, patted the LeMat at his side, and snapped the reins, sending him and the horse back in the direction Cherub had come. He didn't know where the boy had come from or how he got to Cocytus, but Lloyd would keep riding until he made it back home.

# CALAMITY COMPLETE

**SAMUEL AND PAIMON** stood on shaky legs and slowly made their way to where Lycus's house had stood moments ago. The remaining two members of The Calamity Three watched a giant beast rip through the sky, swallow the house, and continue crashing through the earth, but when they stood at the edge of the crater it was only three or four feet deep. The men deduced the monster must've fallen through the same kind of opening it fell out of, otherwise they'd be staring down an infinitely deeper chasm.

"Well," Samuel started. "What do you reckon we do now?"

"I think I have an idea," said a gravelly voice from behind the bandits.

The men whirled around as fast as their injuries would allow and drew on the stranger sneaking up on them, but quickly lowered their guns when they saw it was the third member of their crew. The one who was dead. Even though the men had put Luke in the ground hours earlier, there was no denying it was him standing right there in front of them. He was filthy with the dirt they'd buried him under, and his eyes had a strange glow to them, but he otherwise seemed no worse for the wear.

"L—L—Luke?" Samuel stammered and scratched his head with the barrel of his gun. "That you?"

"Well, it ain't your whore mother!" Luke growled the words more than spoke them. "You wanna know what we're gonna do now, boys?"

Samuel and Paimon exchanged quick glances and nodded.

"We're gonna take this town for ourselves and make sure every last son-of-a-bitch in Cocytus knows about it. Now, before we get started, give me back my goddamn boots!"

# ACKNOWLEDGEMENTS

Thanks to everyone for always making fun of my name.

# ABOUT THE AUTHOR

John Wayne Comunale lives in the neon-drenched city of sin Las Vegas to prepare himself for the heat in Hell. He is the author of *Death Pacts and Left-Hand Paths, Scummer, As Seen On T.V., Sinkhole, The Cycle* and more. He hosts the weekly storytelling podcast *John Wayne Lied to You* and fronts the punk rock disaster johnwayneisdead. He currently travels around the country giving truly unique and most excellent performances of the written word. Find everything at johnwayneisdead.com

# ALSO BY JOHN WAYNE COMUNALE

Death Pacts and Left-Hand Paths
The Cycle
The Cadillac Man
Sinkhole
Deadline
and more